Gods and Devils

Jason Morgan

A JJ&C Foundation book

Published by JJ&C Foundation Sydney

Gods and Devils

Historical fiction
Germany -- History -- Fiction -- Bibliography

World War, 1939-1945

833.032

Cover illustration: Carl Morgan Zookraft Design

ISBN: 099254680X
ISBN-13: 978-0992546809

DEDICATION

The author dedicates this book to families of holocaust victims

ACKNOWLEDGMENTS

The author would like to acknowledge Jeremy Macpherson and Carl Morgan who assisted in many wonderful ways to this novel.

i

CHAPTER 1

Felix Kersten's life began in 1898, to a mother who was a masseuse with magical hands. Her name was Olga, a postman's daughter. Kersten's grandfather was the French ambassador to the Russian court. He stood in attendance, stiff as a plank while the child was christened in a country church in Dorpat, Estonia. The mood was serious but cheerful. Birds flapped their wings in the church roof. The priest poured water over the infant's skull. Everyone smiled and clapped as though they sensed good things to come. The child however, wriggled restlessly in the priest's arms and screamed at the angels floating in the ceiling.

Years passed and the child continued to rebel. He spent idle hours in his classroom thinking about food and dozing at his desk. His appetite for gourmet food became prestigious. Notorious even. His body filled out like an expanding loaf. Rolls of lard weighed down his hound dog chin and his monstrous jaws that he kept busy by chewing. His grades suffered. Somehow, he managed to make it into a German school for agriculture in Schleswig-Holstein. Here he kept mostly to himself. He remained captive to the haze of his listless indecision, like a mariner stranded in some ungodly fog.

In 1914 World War broke out. Russia acted on their mistrust of Baltic families like the Kerstens who fled to a small village near the Caspian Sea, where sea spray blew over their brick chimneys and squalls rattled their window shutters. No longer could Kersten communicate with his parents. For the first time in his life, he felt alone. He realized then, under the blow of necessity evoked by war, that he needed his family. He would fight for them, like they had fought for him with their patience and love. The listless child was no more. Only his famous appetite remained.

Kersten joined a Finnish resistance group that fought German domination in their homeland. After 1919, when Brest Listo signed a peace treaty, the Kerstens united. It was the first time Kersten had seen his parents for years. They sang and got drunk on red wine (except for Kersten who had never drunk in his life). They laughed and reminisced long into the night. Kersten's father Frederick fell asleep snoring in his armchair with his pipe still dangling from his mouth. Olga threw a blanket over him, tucking it beneath his chin, and kissed his wrinkled forehead.

For a time things were going well. Kersten continued his services. Yet something-some destiny-some trigger in his genes eluded his knowledge and kept him from happiness. A bubble that simmered at the surface but would not break. In short, he remained restless as ever.

After a bout of rheumatism that almost claimed his life, Kersten discovered what his existence was missing. He shook his head at the simplicity of it. He would become a physical therapist, just like his mother Olga was.

Fortune agreed with Kersten's suspicions and latent wishes. The renowned Dr. Kollander agreed to take on the new pupil. Kersten prepared for his trip to Berlin where he would begin training. On the night before his departure he sat down for one last gigantic meal with his parents: an oven based venison roast served with demi-glace sauce, mashed potatoes and wild mushrooms.

That night he was too excited to sleep. He wondered if he had had any choice in choosing this path. Kersten thought how strange life seemed when events seemed inevitable, even after years of trying to flee from them. Far from obstructing their course, even fortune seemed to conspire in their making.

CHAPTER 2

Felix Kersten had almost finished his bowl of pasta when his phone rang. Food was one of his favorite things, yet he showed no anger at this interruption. Kersten was not easily given to hostility. He wiped his mouth with his napkin and ambled to the phone in the corridor, pondering all the while. *The quicker I get this conversation over with, the sooner I can return to my meal.*

Kersten loved all types of food. He liked pork ribs with smoky barbecue ribs, layered pasta cakes and ice cream with root beer sherbet swirl. Most of all he liked creamy cake that spoiled his palate with richness and gave him instant pleasure. He picked up the phone and put it to his ear. 'Hello.'

It was his friend, the German industrialist Rosterg. He sounded desperate and afraid. 'You must come to Berlin immediately.'

Kersten licked a bit of meat sauce from the edge of his mouth. 'Is old Diehn sick? Does he need me?'

Only the slow, monotonous tone of the telephone wires. The insulated copper conductors seemed to have something caught in their throat.

'No. Another friend, the important one I told you about. Remember...'

Kersten's eyes snapped wide and white. He recollected the tea party he had almost a year ago with Rosterg who begged him to take on a new patient. But Kersten had refused, and he even told Rosterg that he alone must save his potash industry from nationalization.

'I want nothing to do with politics. I know nothing about it.'

That is what Kersten had said. His small blue eyes turned a steely, violent hue and Rosterg knew better than to ask again. Until now.

Kersten pondered. His friend sounded devastated. Kersten finally ended the silence with an unusually solemn voice. 'I shall do as you ask.'

Kersten hung up and walked back to the table in utter silence, falling into his chair. He let his meal go cold, staring into space, contemplating a treacherous future he thought he had left long ago.

CHAPTER 3

Berlin flickered like a quietly seething hell. From west to the Knie the 20,000 brown shirts came, holding aloft torches, thudding past in their black boots. From the sky they must have looked like a huge, shining serpent. A river of flames flowing over the darkened streets, stretching far as eyes could see, murmuring ominously against the night.

Kersten was impressed and afraid. The spectacle was terrible and beautiful. It had the strange power of a dream or a medieval spell. The modern world had seen nothing seen like it. He didn't mention these thoughts to his wife Irmgard. She had other things on her mind like his peace of mind. She never expected he would succumb to Rosterg's pleas. But now that he had, she realized she had to support him. 'You've healed Kings, Queens, aristocrats and industrialists. If you cannot assist him, who can?'

Yes, yes, that is what Rosterg said too. Kersten shook his head just thinking about it. It was true, of course. Since he was a child Kersten knew he had an extraordinary sense of touch. He could sooth his dying grandmother simply by touching her waxy forehead or rubbing her gaunt shoulders. Animals flocked to him, as though to feel his touch. As he grew older he developed these strange skills. With his fingers he could tell at once the differences in the thickening of the tissues in different layers of the body.

Irmgard diverted her eyes from the road to her husband. 'Don't worry. You'll be fine. Just be your usual, confidant self.'

'I am.'

'No you're not. You look pale. Put some of that blush on,' Irmgard suggested glancing at the console where her rouge sat. 'It will put colour in your cheeks.'

Kersten gave the faintest laugh. There was no point hiding his fear. He needed to justify to Irmgard why he had taken on this job. He gazed at his wife who looked beautiful in her makeup and flowered hat that she wore tilted over her eyes.

'I owe it to Finland. I will have access to information undreamt of.'

Irmgard sniffed ironically. 'So you're a spy now.'

Kersten kept silent.

'You're not a soldier anymore, Felix. You're a masseur.'

With chin in hand Kersten turned his head back to the window. The wide streets flashed by, along with the Swastika flags draped over storefronts and majestic doorways of museums, council chambers, libraries and theatres. To judge by this display, along with the pictures of Hitler people put up in their windows, Germany was in love with the Führer.

Kersten wanted to be home again at his estate Hartzwalde on the outskirts of Berlin, where he could listen to the wind rustling the wheat grass, now a meter tall at least. He wanted to play with his son, his stomach being an object of reference for the boy who would climb it or pound it innocently with his fist until it hurt.

For the rest of the journey they said nothing at all.

No.8 Prinz Albrecht-Strasse consumed the whole corner of the street. The darkened windows leered like suspicious eyes. Except for those upstairs that had shutters drawn across them. These rooms were where police tortured suspects, way above the street, where no one could hear the screams.

The motor died. Irmgard slumped over the steering wheel, closed her eyes and laid her temple over her white knuckles. Kersten watched her thick eyelashes fluttering. He lifted his corpulent face to stare at the soldiers out the front of the building. They wore black uniforms and helmets that shone, and they marched in a strange formation like wind-up toys, rifles stabbing the cloudless sky. These were the brutes that had been molesting people in the streets for years. It was hard to look at them while the spring sun beat off their iron skulls.

'*These are men.*' Kersten told himself. '*Not monsters.*'

The yawning door of the headquarters was like a mouth. Many who entered it never came out. No wonder civilians passed it quickly or avoided it altogether.

The rest of the street, however, continued mostly like it would have done under any other political party. Cars whirled passed, and common citizens strolled along the footpaths. This normality only added to the strange world that Kersten was entering. He shut the car door, and kissed his wife who told him she loved him.

The building swallowed Kersten. He stood for a moment in awe like a mouse in the jaws of some great beast. The grey stone building had sparse corridors, gaping arches and polished wooden bannisters. It did not take long for someone to notice him. An officer squeezed into a helmet which came down over his eyebrows approached Kersten who told the soldier he needed to see the Reichsführer. The man's face remained calm as stone as he left Kersten to report the matter. While Kersten signed a piece of paper another guard, extremely tall, stood over him with a rifle. Two stylized lightning bolts were embroidered on his broad shoulder blades. When Kersten was finished he looked up and lifted his fedora to the lieutenant. A monocle stuck in the man's pallid face like an old coin put there to pay the ferryman.

'Follow me.'

Kersten held one of these bannisters as he mounted the marble stairs, one step at a time. Couriers, officers and orderlies went up and down the steps in busy but precise motion. All wore immaculate SS uniforms with rifles slung over their shoulders. Those who bothered to look at him did so mistrustfully as though he were an alien. Kersten, however, had more serious concerns. In a few moments he would meet the monster who many Germans feared more than Hitler.

CHAPTER 4

The man had passed out minutes ago. The SS officer threw water over the prisoner's head, and he dragged his eyes open. Two cracked stones in his gaunt skull. Water ran from his hair, and from the tip of his nose. The three officers stood back and watched. One of them laughed, bearing his teeth. The prisoner was naked astride a vice on a bench that crushed his testicles which had turned blue. His hands were handcuffed behind his back. His feet were gory and black from where the police had burnt him with soldering-lamps and plunged a knife into his flesh. A strand of bloody saliva hung from the man's swollen lips. He swayed drunkenly, spitting blood down his shirt.

Someone knocked at the door. Himmler nodded to one of his men to answer it. The door opened and a young guard appeared. 'Herr Himmler, the doctor is here,' he said, not even looking at the prisoner, for torture had long since become common practice.

Himmler had talked to Kersten once for two minutes when he rang the doctor to confirm the appointment. He smiled. 'I mustn't keep the good doctor waiting.'

Heinrich Himmler had opened the office door before Kersten had even arrived. The Reichsführer studied Kersten from behind his spectacles that he pushed to the bridge of his nose. He was as far from the Nordic god he idealised than could be imagined. He was small, stooped over and had cynical grey eyes. His broad cheekbones seemed oriental like his round face which looked as weary as his unimpressive body. His eyebrows that were thick as wires almost covered his eyes. His head was strongly domed but not high as though someone had hit him with a shovel. His weak chin receded like the mouth of a shark. He was pinched and pale with pupils so small Kersten barely saw them. The mouth was soft but ended abruptly and stubble dotted his jowls. *This is a face*, Kersten thought, *lacking any substantial structure*.

In Germany, only Hitler was more powerful.

'Please, sit' Himmler said gesturing with an open hand to the seat opposite him. 'Karl Wolff tells me you're the finest.'

'I do my best,' Kersten replied, sinking into the chair while finding it hard to remove his eyes from the insignificant looking man before him. Later, Kersten would discover that many officers laughed at the man's weak appearance while living in fear of his power. There was, however, good reason to dread this man. He had a faultless record. His Gestapo exercised the first line of disciplinary control over Germany.

Himmler sniffed, wriggled his dainty moustache, and consulted some papers on his desk. As he read through them, Kersten observed the light from the open window reflecting on Himmler's spectacles. All was silent save from the rustle of papers that Himmler turned over in his delicate hands. Kersten sat at attention.

'You have an impressive régime for our regime. '

Kersten thought this was a play on words and began to laugh. The dark line of Himmler's facial hair descended. Kersten stopped abruptly.

'You fought in the First World War and assisted in the Finnish Civil war. You became second lieutenant in the Finnish army, studied under Dr. Kollander who showed great faith in you. So much in fact, that he turned all his patients over to you. One of whom was Prince Hendrik in the Netherlands.'

Himmler drew a long dissatisfied breath through his nose. He snorted with contempt, studying the file in his hand. Kersten sat as he usually did, with his plump hands resting on his huge stomach. Himmler barely knew him, yet already he felt an amiable kindness emanate from the man with the magic hands.

'I've always sided with tough hot blooded Southerners myself, the working man.' Himmler said. 'Men of the soil. That is doubtlessly where the German people gain their vigor.'

He put the paper down beside him and studied Kersten. 'I come from the soil,' he said thoughtfully, leaning back touching his fingers together. 'I was a chicken farmer. But because I'm not ashamed of it, no one bothers to embarrass me about it. I believe it's nobler to be a good peasant than a treacherous aristocrat. Better to earn your honor than inherit it.'

Himmler pondered his words while Kersten nodded positively. The Reichsführer picked the page back up and scrawled down it with his piggy eyes until he stopped. 'You worked as a dish washer then as a film extra to make ends meet here in Germany. Hmmm…'

Kersten shrugged his broad shoulders and smiled bashfully.

'But that is what the English call academic at this point.' Himmler continued, throwing down the folder. 'Can you cure me?'

'Cure is too stronger word, Herr Himmler.'

'Yes, what I meant was, can you relieve me.'

Himmler leant forward and looked Kersten straight in the eye.

'Sometimes my pain is so bad I pass out. Do you know how that must look to my men?'

Himmler leant back and pondered, cupping his frail chin.

'I'll try anything. The Führer does. He suffers similar unbearable stomach cramps. Since 1936 he's been taking capsules derived from the bacteria found in the excrement of a Bulgarian peasant.'

Kersten lifted his eyebrows.

'I don't think much of Dr. Morrell, and many of his esteemed peers share my doubts. But enough of the small talk. Can you help me?'

Kersten had seen many powerful men brought to their knees with pain so Himmler's urgency did not surprise him. 'Firstly, I will have to acquaint myself with your body. In two weeks I will know if I can help you. But only after that.'

Himmler nodded. 'Let's get started then, shall we.'

Himmler stripped to his waist and sat on the divan. He was thin chested with shoulders narrower than his flabby torso. His belly rolled down in pale waves of blubber. He removed his thin framed spectacles that he placed on his table while he laid down. 'What happen to your teacher?'

'Dr. Ko?'

'Yes...'

'One day I visited him and he told me, 'Kersten, I only have eight years to live.' The Lamas had pinpointed this date on his horoscope when he was a boy. I've never saw him since. I don't think I ever will.'

Himmler smiled with polite amusement. Kersten smiled too for the memory of his old master brought warmth to his heart. But Himmler didn't smile for long. He began to wince with pain as Kersten explored the Reichsführer's flesh beneath his heavy, small fingers that were so powerful they had cured almost all they had touched.

Kersten located the points of pain on Himmler's body without having to hear a word. His sensitive fingers did not cure by calming or stimulating the patient by manual pressure or the use of vibrations. His method was different. He penetrated the skin, soothing the sub-cutaneous and muscular tissues. He relaxed the nerves.

"See with a feeling eye, feel with a seeing hand."

Calmly and silently, Kersten kneaded Himmler's flesh like a loving baker. Laid out on the bed almost naked, Himmler looked like someone sunbathing, or a man who had been shot. Sometimes he sighed. As his pain oozed away he felt euphoria rescuing him, and even time and space seemed to vanish. The success was immediate, but painful. Himmler gritted his teeth in agony, writhing and crying into the divan. Kersten had long known about anatomy and physiology. He forced the good blood to the heart and the bad blood away from it. The blood renewed itself more rapidly, nourishing the tissues and muscles. Finally, Kersten dropped Himmler's arms. The Reichsführer paused as though to observe the miracle he had experienced. He placed his feet on the floor, delicately, as though not to disrupt the fragility of his newly found peace. He behaved like someone made of the most delicate and fragile glass that would shatter at any second. Yet his face was calm, beatified and flushed with life that Kersten had circulated with his fingers and palms. Himmler felt as though he had emerged from a different world and it took him a moment to recognise himself. He tried to imagine what had happened to him, yet judging by his face, Kersten knew Himmler had no notion. Beads of sweat stood out on Himmler's forehead. 'I believe you and I, Mr Kersten, will become the best of friends.'

CHAPTER 5

The weeks passed. Many SS soldiers regarded the fat, friendly man who passed through their doors with contempt and even suspicion. Kersten, for most part ignored them. His mind remained focused on the Reichsführer. Already, Kersten was becoming familiar with not only Himmler's body, but his mind.

'So do you agree to take me on, Herr Kersten?' Himmler asked from his desk, watching Kersten sit across from him.

'Yes. I ask only for a few conditions. One, I don't want to join any political organisation. Two, I will treat you like I do any other patient, except I will come to you. Three, I can come and go as I please.'

Himmler nodded. Then he reached and shook Kersten's hand.

'You have a deal, my little Buddha.'

Kersten arrived as soon as the embassy doors opened to meet with Finnish ambassador Toivo Mikael Kivimaki for help. The bald man with the proud moustache was less helpful than Kersten had expected. He snorted and sat looking at Kersten with his palms spread across his desk below the window that overlooked Berlin.

'Your native Estonia is annexed with the Soviets who you had fought against, and who will kill you quicker than it takes for your blood to dry on their bayonets. The Dutch Nazis are envious and suspicious of you. I suggest you stay where you are serving Himmler. Believe it or not, that is where you're safest. Under the dragon's wing. It is also where you can best serve Finland. I want you to report to Helsinki whenever possible. You got this far by being a professional. Nothing needs to change.'

Kersten was afraid. He lowered his head as though his doubts were weighing him down. He wondered if this was worth sacrificing himself for. Yet Kolo had taught Kersten confidence and self-belief. Although the doctor didn't want to admit it, Kivimaki's request flattered him.

~

At the end of the day's treatment Kersten moved towards the door when he heard Himmler call. He had noticed that something was on Himmler's mind.

'By the way, Kersten…'

'Yes.'

'War is about to start.'

11

Kersten felt the air desert the room. He felt like he was choking, and his face went pale although he knew this was going to happen all along.

'You and your family must leave Holland and come to live in Germany. Only here can I promise your safety.'

Kersten returned home late to his home in Holland. He placed his coat on the hook and went into the darkened lounge room where he slumped on the couch running his hands across his face in the silence. Irmgard stood in the doorway, but even from there she saw him stooped and depressed. Like a mountain caving into a black sea.

'What's wrong?' she asked blinking in the pale light. Kersten held his forehead as though he were holding up something made of stone.

'We must leave for Germany. The war has started.'

CHAPTER 6

Before Kersten had had his visa processed he received a call from his patient. 'You cannot have your visa. You must stay in Germany.' Himmler said. Kersten held the phone tighter to his ear and waited for his horror to pass but it would not. He feared he was seeing the beginning of something terrible he could not yet imagine. 'I will go to the Finnish embassy.'

Himmler roared laughing. 'If I can't help you they won't. I request you stay at your estate for the coming week. Do not leave it.'

Kersten went pale. 'Then I'm a prisoner.'

'Think whatever you choose. But rest assured-Finland will not declare war for your sake.'

The next two weeks were the most anxious of Kersten's life. His family barely left his Hartzwalde mansion. Gloomy silence pervaded the house that became quiet as a monastery. Not even the serenity of the woods or the murmuring brooks offered him calm. He tried to think of nothing. He dangled his feet in the stream watching the ripples and water fleeing over pebbles and rocks towards the rivers that awaited them with open embraces. At night he played chess with his maid and the woman he thought of as his sister, Elizabeth Lube. Irmgard and he would listen to records and the radio or play with the baby. But these distractions were fleeting. He worried about his homeland and how the SS would ravage through it without remorse. He knew from whispers about the atrocities they committed. He wondered how he could serve Finland as he had promised: from the devil's lair.

The fourteenth day came and went. The phone rang out early in the morning and woke Kersten. He reached out of bed and held the receiver to his ear while he struggled to accustom himself to the light.

'Pack your bags,' the voice said. 'The Reichsführer needs you on board his private train tomorrow.'

~

The black locomotive was Himmler's headquarter on wheels with sleeping, dining and parlour cars. Behind it trailed the devil's smoke that brought hunger, torture and death wherever it went. The train stopped at Flamersfeld in Waterland. Kersten was in his apartment where he pressed his face against the window through which he watched the SS agents pour out like spiders scuttling along a web. They scurried far and wide down the mouths of diverging streets. Kersten lowered his face, shading his eyes with his hand in grim silence. A knock at his door.

'Come in.'

'My dear Kersten, come with me and watch us beat the French.'

'I am not a military man. I do not enjoy seeing cities go up in flames.'

'War is necessary. The Führer said so.'

Himmler was made very happy by Hitler's words, and he believed them as if they had been spoken by an oracle.

'Maybe next time. I need to rest.'

That evening Kersten tried to sleep but could not. He heard the drunken cheers, the crude toasts and howls of men celebrating France's downfall like jackals howling over a carcass. Liquor mounted their heads while their minds descended. Kersten turned over on his side. His stomach growled with hunger but he could not bring himself to eat.

The next day was better for he met and spoke with Rudolf Brandt, Himmler's secretary, who he invited into his compartment where they shared creamy cake and strong coffee. Brandt was about forty like Kersten, and with his plain intellectual face framed by spectacles he almost resembled his superior. Kersten thought it was narcissistic for Himmler to have hired a lookalike, but he wasn't surprised. Himmler's ego was great as his fear. Yet unlike other Nazis, and many people observed this, he often seemed refined, quietly noble and modest while so many of his colleagues were bold and arrogant. Kersten realised if he related to Himmler at all, it was because of these personality traits.

'I hear you have magic hands and that you saved Prince Hendrik when the doctors said he could live no longer than six months.'

'I'm only doing what I've been taught. I was just lucky to have a great master...'

Brandt put his cup down on his saucer while his face darkened. 'I must warn you as a friend, that men in the SS are after you. They believe you're an agent.'

Kersten bit his lip. 'Misery breeds guile...'

The days passed. Kersten grew bored. He briefly visited the nearby village where he saw children chasing SS jeeps along the road. Their tyre tracks remained in the mud while clouds of blue exhaust smoke hung in the air. When he wasn't eating and drinking coffee Kersten went hunting for mushrooms. One day he saw a white dress hanging from a wire strung up between two sycamores in an abandon backyard. He stood studying it. The sun was setting. The air smelt moist and the ground was dampening beneath his feet. Kersten plodded back to the carriage with his tub of mushrooms. Like some innocent traveller lost among the woods in a grim fairy-tale.

The next day he wandered the train and chose to explore Himmler's library in one of the cars. He paced before the shelves of books with an air of quiet judgment, and his arms pinned behind his back as though browsing one of the art galleries that he loved to visit. Himmler's collection surprised Kersten. It included the Old Testament, The Gospels, The Koran and mystical texts along with historical books on religion and law. He was scanning his eyes over them when he heard Himmler enter the room. Kersten turned and glanced at the Reichsführer who was still glowing about Germany's easy victory of France.

'You told me Nazis have no religion.'

'These are only for my work.' Himmler replied. 'We must understand the enemy. The Führer said 'you cannot get around the concept of God.' He is always right. Now he has given me a special task: to write a new bible of the Germanic faith. Christ will eventually fade from history. When future generations pray it shall be Hitler's name they murmur.'

Kersten unfolded his arms.

'One day, the Führer will have his long hoped for wish…'

'Which is…?'

'To replace every Catholic school room crucifix with pictures of him…'

CHAPTER 7

Martine.

North of Paris everyone deserted the towns and the crops rotted in the dirt, most of them devoured by the first wave of German troops who left corpses of animals and men to rot on the open ground. Naked skulls of cows, pigs and sheep left with their dull blue eyes that seemed to glare still. Stiff bodies of deer on blood caked earth expanding in the heat. Flies crawling over their dead gentle eyes and in their gaping mouths. Corpses dangled from the trees, their feet jostling stiffly from side to side, their gory chins resting on their chests, eyelids closed in dreamless sleep, the wheatgrass beneath them, blood-soaked.

Martine met her friend, Francisco, in the coffee shop. They wanted to relieve their suffering so they ordered chocolate cake along with their Lattes. They talked in energetic whispers. Francisco told Martine that the people of Malines saw Nazis marching the British east. The prisoners filed past mournfully like vaudeville performers or brutalised clowns, driven from some strange fun park, filth drying in their hair and streaking their faces. The Nazis had ridiculed them by making them wear plumed women's caps and bonnets strapped to their hairy chins.

'God knows what they'll do to us.' Martine told her friend, stirring her coffee. She was a primary school teacher, small, dark and plain with shoulder length hair. Francisco was prettier, fair with smiling green eyes.

Martine knew about the Nazis and she hated them. Her hatred maybe even exceeded her fear. That is one reason why she kept a Jewess and her two small children in her attic. It was not safe for them even there. But the shock of such a rapid invasion had taken everyone by surprise. People walked the streets with stunned indifference. It took only six weeks for Europe's greatest army to capitulate. On the day the Nazis entered Paris, sixteen Parisians took their lives. Many more had succumbed to the Gestapo. These cases were kept secret but rumours found their way out. The Nazis did all they could to extract information from Parisians. Behind the sound proof walls of torture rooms the officers blindfolded their victims and whipped them mercilessly. Others were bound to stakes and shot so many times their bodies became sieves while others were burned alive in chambers where fingers stiffened in their last agony left marks on the walls.

Martine didn't tell even her closes friends her secret. Nor did she tell her family because she feared the burden of this knowledge was far too great.

The coffee shop the girls met at was one of the few left. Most buildings were empty shells. Only the trains contained life, which they sped constantly away from this ghost city. Many passengers had no destinations.

Food was scarce, a problem not only for Martine but for her captive friends too. Martine was contemplating this very thought, when she rose to leave. Not a moment too soon either. A horde of German soldiers had strolled into the café. The older customers nodded them a wary good evening. The Gestapo followed their gaze. The waitresses began flirting with them, leaning over the counter to parade their cleavage, smiling and stroking their hair. Two of the officers had young women with them who spoke French. They cooed and kissed the officer's ears while their men rubbed their behinds and along their thighs.

'I'll see you soon, Francisco. Don't worry. Everything will be fine. Maybe all you need is a German boyfriend…'

Martine took the long way home. She passed the carnival where only weeks ago mothers had taken their children to play. How strange it now seemed. Rides like the Thriller and the Moonrocket seemed to be dead or sleeping. The merry go round pigs stared at her eerily from their golden poles. She caught herself staring in one of the fun mirrors that bent and twisted her as though a black hole were stretching her. In the distance she saw the sea heaving onto the shore like a vast sleeping beast. How often Martine had sat on that beach with her heels dug in the sand watching the tide wash up upon her bare feet. She would not visit it now and may never do so again. Everything that reminded her of the old world brought more pain than joy. She finally reached the end of the silent, deserted fairground. Sea breeze beating a canvas tent. The world boomed in the wind. At Martine's feet lay a French flag hauled down from one of the canvas marquees. She walked on. The streets were almost as quiet. Bare. She strode along the townhouses that seemed more like prisons. Many of them empty. Most civilians had gathered their belongings and were choking the roads like ragged gypsies but Martine did not think that it would safe for the family she sheltered to join them. What if the German soldiers saw them? They would have shot them where they stood.

Martine passed many German soldiers but barely glanced at any of them. Some were unrolling Nazi flags and draping them over buildings. Wind followed her, rushing at her back, booming in her ears. It scattered dead leaves about her ankles. A Swastika flag lashed spitefully in the gale. When she turned into her street she saw SS sitting at their jeeps, pointing and arguing with each other. She was sick with worry for the young family who she had known since she was a child. The Jewess's husband had left her, which made things even harder for her. Martine promised Levana that no danger would come to her or her daughters. 'Why would the Nazis interfere with me?' Martine laughed bravely. 'I'm a thirty three year old single primary school teacher. I would think they'd pity me more than anything.'

Martine had only just stepped inside and went to get herself a glass of water from the tap when she heard someone ring the doorbell. At once she ran up the stairs and opened the attic door. Inside it was dark and musty.

'Quick, you must hide in the cavity,' she whispered loudly, and her three friends scuttled along the floor like frightened rats, their eyes pale and wide with horror.

Martine hurried downstairs.

'Wait, I'm coming,' she cried to the doorbell that rang again. When she pulled the small chain across she peered through the crack and saw three men dressed in black with swastika armbands. The oldest one in the middle was tall and he had a grey face. The men behind him looked thirty and held rifles. The oldest who was obviously in charge, spoke in French.

'Martine Belrose. I'm police sergeant Florian Amsel. Do you mind if we come in?'

'No, of course not.'

Martine opened the door and the men entered one at a time. Their black boots echoed on the wooden boards. Light chink of steel. The officers glanced in both directions. Martine sunk back, clasping her hands in front of her waist. 'Is something wrong?' she asked.

Florian studied her with his grey eyes. 'I hope not.'

'Would you and your men like a -'

'Search the house,' Florian said before inspecting his watch. 'I would like to finish so I can party with those Parisian tarts everyone tells me about.'

The soldiers seemed to have done this many times before. They searched methodically, looking for who Martine guessed were the Cohens. While she slunk in the corner Florian paced around with his hands behind his back and his chest out, picking up photos of Martine's parents that she kept on the mantel piece above a fire that hadn't worked for years. He walked a few more laps of the tiny lounge before removing a list from his trousers.

'These cafés and bars, so people tell me, are popular with ladies. I will read them and you can give me your educated opinion which one best suits its reputation.'

When Florian finished reading the list, he paused. Martine's breath snagged in her throat. Eventually, she stuttered. 'The second last one.'

Florian stroked his chin thoughtfully.

'It's rather wild. That's if you're looking for that type of place.'

Florian sat like a rock. He cleared his throat and laid the note on the coffee table and frowned at it. 'Hmm. You seem nervous. I hope we haven't interrupted you. Why are you still here, anyway?'

Martine shook her head to show she didn't know. Florian remained doubtful. They both heard footsteps and then saw the soldiers at the archway. They shook their heads and grunted something in German. Martine listened to the silence. Florian continued to deliberate. 'Have a nice evening, Martine.'

Florian touched his hat and led his men through the door. Only when Martine heard the gate clank shut did she breathe freely. She waited a few moments before heading to the window where she parted the curtain and peered outside. The men were no longer in sight. She strolled deliberately to the closet in her room that she shoved aside. She opened the secret door of the cavern behind it. The family were terrified and they surfaced, pale and stinking of fear. They shrivelled against the dying day light that lit up their black eyes. The children would not let go of their mother who tried to be strong. But she was also trembling.

'Come.' Martine said wrapping her arms around them and ushering them through the room. 'Let's all drink some water.'

The three of them sat silently around the kitchen. Bees buzzed outside the kitchen window. Everyone looked haggard and tired and they drank with despair in their eyes that gazed at the emptiness before them. Then they began to laugh, at first only slightly. But soon they laughed until they shuddered.

'We did it,' Martine cried, tears of triumph rolling down her cheeks. 'I know. I can't believe it.' Levana said, putting her hand to her mouth. 'Blockhead Germans.'

'The war will end soon.' Martine said reaching across the table to squeeze Levana's hand. 'America will join the allies. They have too much industry for the German's to fight against.'

Levana tried to smile, but her pity and fear would not allow it. 'Yes, you're right Marty. And if not the Americans then those resourceful Russians. We know how tough they are, don't we children?'

Levana smiled at her son and daughter and so did Martine. But not for long. The doorbell buzzed again. This time Martine didn't have to say anything. The family shuffled on their small feet back to the cavity with Martine ambling closely behind. When she answered the door she looked out of breath.

'Martine.' Florian smiled. 'I left my list behind.'

Martine stood aside and the sergeant entered. He glanced about and put his nose to the air as though he smelt something suspicious. Martine looked through the front door and saw his two men leaning against a tree in the fallen leaves, smoking. They peered up at her from the shadows of their helmets before continuing their conversation. She imagined her friends sheltering in the darkness, breathing heavily with their eyes closed.

When he had pushed the note back into his pocket, the sergeant lifted his eyes at Martine who leaned in the doorway with her arms folded. Florian paused.

'Could I trouble you with a glass of water?'

'Of course.'

Martine led Florian into the kitchen where he passed again, but this time with surprise. At first, Martine had no idea why. But then she saw what caught his eye.

'Four glasses that were not there only a moment ago. And one person.'

'My neighbours visited.'

'For a whole three minutes then hurried through the back door. I think not.'

A fly that was crawling over the lip of one glass slid down the inside and started to drown in the dregs of water at the bottom.

Florian walked into the hallway and summoned his men with a wave of his hand. Martine sat at the kitchen table, lowering her eyes while the men stormed inside swinging their chins about. They searched more violently this time, throwing furniture aside, ripping books from the shelves, upturning beds and hauling down cabinets and closets. Barely anything survived this savage scrutiny. Perfume bottles and vases smashed at their feet or rolled clanking on the floorboards. The worse thing, the thing Martine would never forget, was the children crying when the Gestapo found them.

Florian raised his pistol from his holster and aimed it at Martine. She heard him cock it. She said nothing at all but sat staring at him hatefully, hard as a stone.

'I could shoot you and no one would punish me. Some would even pin a medal to my chest.' Martin lowered the hammer. 'This is too lovelier place for you to die.'

Florian put the gun back into its holster, went to the door and made a trumpet with his hands. 'I have business here,' he yelled. 'I will see you at headquarters.' The guards nodded and took the family who had to clasp their hands behind their heads. The Cohens gazed about. As though there was someone there to help them. The Gestapo pressed down their skulls and lowered them into the black car. Martine wanted to shriek at them, but she could not even do that. The cry stuck in her throat. Instead she sobbed like a child.

Florian shut the door, seized Martine's arm, and led her into the kitchen where he tore down her panties, bent her over the table, unbuckled his trousers and raped her.

~

The guards herded the prisoners inside the train carriages like cattle. Martine thought they would have to drag her kicking and screaming into the container. But this was not so. She surprised herself at how she normalised this tragedy. She didn't even cry although she felt like it.

The SS grunted at them like apes, lifting their lips above their teeth, pushing them along. Martine shuffled towards the carriage. One guard spat in her face as she climbed inside the container.

Martine glared wildly about as darkness filled with people pressing against her. She listened to the old people and the children sucking at the air. This cramped carriage of human flesh would be their home for two weeks or more. Some would probably perish before they reached camp. A solitary bucket was placed in the corner to shit and piss in.

Soon the carriage reeked of urine and excrement. All day long she heard moans and tears. Some fainted with hunger and others descended into craziness, repeating phrases or praying to the blackness which was the world entire.

CHAPTER 8

Kersten's ability to relieve Himmler's excruciating stomach cramps opened up doors through which he saw the internal workings of the Reich. Kersten witnessed up close the arteries and veins at its black heart.

The Reichsführer referred Kersten to other party members. Himmler believed Kersten could test the nervous energy and reactions of his officers. Thus Himmler could access their minds.

Among the new patients, was Dr Robert Ley, leader of the Deutsche Arbeitis. He was as ugly as his wife was Nordic, tall and beautiful. One day Kersten arrived at the doctor's mansion and found the man drunk, like he was so often. He waved Kersten in and offered him a drink from the open bourbon bottle that he filled his glass with in the lounge. Two little poodles jumped at Kersten's ankles, flourishing their tails.

'Get rid of these poodles for Christ sake, Eva.' Robert yelled at the aging house maid who ran in, scooped up the dogs and scurried away.

Kersten sat before him on the couch. Robert leaned back in his armchair and yelled until his face went red and veins stood out on his forehead.

'Darling, I need to see you.'

Kersten said nothing while he gazed about at the photos on Robert's wall that showed him escorting his wife at Nazi parades in their Mercedes convertible surrounded by a sea of faces. So many Nazi supporters, cheering and smiling, waving Swastika flags in the sunlight that seemed to sprinkle them with gold. Thousands of saluting arms elevated together in the jovial air bursting with trumpets, drums, cheers and joyous weeping.

Another framed photo showed them sitting front row at the Day of German Art in Munich 1939. Emilie held an umbrella over Robert who was wrapped in a raincoat splashed with water. Robert's wife was stunning, her doll face smiling beneath a cloud of blonde hair that circled her head. A siren out of water. Beside these snaps was a picture of Ley with Hitler listening to Dr Porsche who was explaining to them the people's car, the KdF wagen. Next to this photograph was a Swastika flag draped across the wall. While Kersten sat studying it with his hands on his knees, he heard the clatter of high heels. Emilie came in. She rolled her blue eyes at her drunken husband.

'Come sit on your husband's lap. The good doctor is here.'

Robert's sad drooping face lit up while his wife sunk into his lap. No sooner had she done so then he began ripping her delicate white dress from her shoulders, exposing her breasts.

'She's beautiful. You must see more of her.'

Emilie sobbed. 'Aufhalten, aufhalten!'

Kersten raised his hand. 'Stop this!' he yelled at Robert who was frothing. 'Cease man, or I will inform Himmler of your behaviour '

Robert sunk to his knees and drooled. Emilie scrambled from the room sobbing, clutching her dress to her breasts. *So these men rule our destiny*, Kersten thought with anger, disgust and even a touch of exasperated humour.

'Please Kersten, don't say anything. That would ruin my career.'

Kersten put his face to his hand. No matter what the Germans did they remained the same barbarians they had always been. He had never known people more incapable of amusing themselves than them. Perhaps, this explained the means they went to hurt others, and ultimately themselves.

Kersten kept Robert's secret. Instead he talked with Himmler on the values of natural medicine, a subject that both men found interesting. As usual, Himmler began preaching like a philosopher on the virtues of natural treatments when someone knocked at his door. It was Reinhard Heydrich, The Blonde Beast, all 191 centimetres of him. Sometimes he interrupted treatments with his messages. Only the Reichsführer wielded more power in the SS. Himmler turned to Kersten who was sitting at Himmler's desk.

'Herr Kersten. Why don't we continue our conversation over dinner this Thursday evening? And I must show you my books on natural medicine. You will love them. My men and I will pick you up at six.'

'That sounds like an idea.'

That night Irmgard almost laughed when she heard the news. The family had sat for dinner over plates of steaming roast vegetables and pork.

'Next he'll invite you on hunting trips.'

Kersten bent over his plate and began shovelling carrots into his mouth. 'Now that will never happen. The man has no stomach for it. He can't understand why we harm animals. I asked why he didn't become vegetarian like Hitler and he said Indian holy teachings permitted eating animals that one hadn't intended killing oneself.'

'Was he right?'

'Yes. He's well read.'

Irmgard rolled her eyes. All that could be heard was the clatter of knives and forks scraping plates. Irmgard stared at Kersten for a moment and then tossed her head back and roared laughing.

'Now what is it?' Kersten asked.

'I'm just remembering a story you told me about Adolf Hitler.'

'Which one?'

'The 8th of November 1923 when he spoke at Munich Hall.'

'What?' their son, Ulf asked.

'Adolf Hitler went to a Munich hall where he was guest speaker.' Kersten explained. 'He came dressed like a waiter. He jumped onto a chair and shot a hole in the roof and cried 'revolution'.'

The boy frowned at his father. Irmgard started laughing again, putting down her fork that she had raised as though she were wielding Hitler's pistol. She pictured a young Hitler with his black hair plastered flat to one side of his skull, pointing his pistol at the roof where his bullet had landed, while he shouted from behind his abrupt moustache.

Kersten studied his wife who laughed until she cried. He agreed with her yet her laughter still sounded malicious to him, mocking even. The organisation that paid him was ordered to kill people for such bold behaviour. And they had even used children young as Ulf to report it.

CHAPTER 9

Himmler arrived at six in the evening as planned. His idling black Mercedes Benz W150/770K Coupe was polished so brightly you could shave in its reflection. Himmler sat in the back behind his chauffeur. The SS leader waved at Kersten who trotted down the front steps of his house. The sun was still drifting high above the oak trees. The still air was warm and fragrant. It smelt of grass and flowers.

Kersten sat beside his boss who smiled and asked him how his family were. Nothing seemed to warm Himmler's heart more than conservative institutions like family and marriage. This didn't stop him however, from enjoying his tight skirted secretaries.

While they chatted the driver remained silent from behind his black skulled cap. Kersten couldn't remember such flattering uniforms in all of history. Himmler acknowledged this to Kersten. 'Clothes must suit the profession or position that one follows,' he said. The SS leader also knew the enhancing effect it had on men. His subordinates aspired to its dramatic mythology like they aspired to their leader's pledge of rural Utopias, great farming estates, awaiting them after their years of service. They too, like their heroic Nordic ancestors, could return to the grandeur of the soil. Such were their childish, naive romanticism, Kersten had more than once thought. Himmler believed in such notions maybe more than anyone else, and he had done so since his childhood. Yet the Reichsführer knew something else, infinitely more important: many Germans believed in these myths too.

They drove on. *This is what power feels like, primal and exhilarating.* Kersten thought, glancing at Himmler. *No one to taunt or overlook you. Man is born to make a God of himself.*

'So how is your son, Kersten?'

Kersten was about to speak when something caught Himmler's eye from outside the window. 'Stop, stop.' The driver pulled to the curb, and without explanation Himmler leapt outside. Kersten, invigorated with intrigue, followed closely behind. At last, Kersten saw the object of Himmler's frenzied arousal.

'My dear, you must be so proud.' Himmler gushed to the mother, looking down at the small blonde blue-eyed boy squeezing her hand. Both were breathless with shock. They had been waking innocently along the street when Himmler had swooped upon them like an eagle. The Reichsführer's face turned pale. Kersten had seen the leader's go like that when he had shown off his paintings of Aryan heroes, sires of old, brandishing swords or standing proudly at the helm of Viking ships. The boy had no idea what was happening. His mother trembled, but she obviously recognised Himmler, and tried bravely to smile.

The Reichsführer was actually shivering with joy bordering on euphoria. Himmler bent on one knee, clasped the boy's shoulders and gazed into his eyes. 'Behold Kersten: the future of Germany.'

When Himmler finally returned from his enchantment, Kersten could have sworn the Reichsführer's eyes were welling with tears. But he did not stop there. Himmler removed from his waist coat a notepad and a pencil. 'Now if I could just get your name and number.' Himmler said, and the woman obliged. Afterwards, Himmler rustled the boy's hair.

'One day you will be a fine SS soldier.'

Kersten did not mention the incident the next day at Himmler's treatment. But he told Brandt.

The men were drinking lemon tea in the staff room. When Brandt heard the story his eyes lit up.

'Not so long ago Himmler visited a seaport. I'm sure you've noticed he is not one to stay bound his desk. Like many smallish men, including the Führer himself, Heinrich has great energy. He likes to get around. Anyway, he saw a striking young man, the perfect Aryan, handsome, tall and strong. He approached the docker and said; 'You're going to join my Warfen SS. Have you seen service?' The man said he had and Himmler asked, 'What rank? Private, of course. It's always the same. People like this are never promoted in the army. Make a note of this, Brandt: from now on this man is a corporal in the SS.' After turning away from me he looked back at the docker and said; 'You will report at once as personally promoted by me to be SS Unterscharführer in Adolf Hitler's bodyguards. We will arrange the details.'

As requested the man supplied his papers that staff examined. Then he had a medical check. Something strange then happened. We began sending anonymous complaint letters. It seemed the blonde man worked in the bawdy trade and had often been to prison!'

The friends threw back their heads and laughed and only ceased when they heard the crisp ring of leather boots.

'And what's so funny, boys?' the tall, blonde man asked standing in the doorway with his hands pinned behind his slender back.

'Nothing Heydrich. We were just laughing about the pomposity of narrow minded medical practitioners our boss dislikes as much as we.' Brandt replied quickly. Kersten nodded and finished his tea.

Kersten used what remained of a mild, sunny evening to write in his diary. He sat in his study where he could look out upon the oak trees. Wind was kidnapping some orphan leaves outside his window, scattering them to the four corners of the earth.

Gods and Devils

'I made use of Himmler's favourable mood today and proposed that he move a homosexual SS officer abroad on some mission or other. Himmler had threatened to imprison him, and, if the man didn't change, which he promised to me he wouldn't then Himmler would send him to the concentration camp. 'Under no circumstances, Herr Kersten" Himmler replied. 'Enemy intelligence makes great use of homosexuals.'

Apparently, Heydrich had told him that…

Himmler again returned to the matter, glad to have a way out from the unpleasant decision. He told me he would give the boy to his Norwegian staff. But even then I could not stop myself from saying to Himmler: 'Would it not interest you, Herr Himmler, to know that our protégé had modelled himself on Frederick 11?'

'What are you implying?' Himmler retorted. 'You don't believe the lies those dirty Jews said to drag our heroes into the mud? I know that his coldness towards his wife is brought forward as evidence. If you looked you could only find indications, no clear and indisputable proof.'

'It might be difficult to prove such a thing.' I objected.

'Then people should keep quiet.' Himmler said, 'and bow in silence before his greatness.'

This talk stayed in my mind for some time.

Kersten put up his pen and rubbed his tired eyes. He raised his mug of coffee to his lips and drank of it. Then he bent over his desk and finished his diary entry.

Himmler only recognises gods and devils.

CHAPTER 10

Much to Dr Rascher's wife delight, Himmler arrived at the altitude chamber at Dachau to witness the experiment. Himmler loved scientific research. As usual the subject was a political criminal that Himmler in his infinite kindness had rounded up for Rascher. Himmler stood before the chamber rocking back and forth on his leather boots, glaring out from under his skull and bones cap through his round spectacles.

The subject in the striped pyjamas was bound to the ceiling of the chamber where he hung forlorn, wilted in his rags. Air was drained from the room to replicate the gaining of about 1000 meters per minute in altitude. The subject wore no oxygen mask and from his steep descent the pain finally became unbearable. He convulsed and struggled for breath and he went blind while his face contorted in agony as he tore at his head with his fingers. He poked his tongue through his foaming mouth and bit it until it bled, and lolling his eyes finally fell unconscious under the crushing weight of pain. That is how the subject spent his last moments. Himmler was most pleased. He rubbed Rascher's shoulder.

'Good work, Rascher. The Luftwaffe will one day thank you and bless you with infinite praise.'

SS officers hauled the man's gaunt, twisted body down. They took him to a room where they removed his brain and washed it under running water for two hours and left it overnight in a refrigerator. The doctors would then observe cranial nerves before dissecting it over an 18 x24 inch wooden cutting board that would not blunt their knives. They manipulated these pieces with forceps which they used to lower the subjects brain into a salad colander lined with cheesecloth. The rest of the criminal was scraped from the floor and taken in garbage bags to an unmarked grave deep in the forest.

Before leaving Dachau, Himmler paid his attention to another experiment that inspired his imagination. Dr Wilhelm Beiglboeck greeted him with adoring eyes, his hands clasped in front of his stomach. He bowed the Reichsführer into a room where emancipated gypsies sustained by sea water alone scurried on all fours licking the floor they had mopped for water. Their eyes were crazed and their shallow breaths filled the air. Himmler could not stand the smell of them, and exited without expression.

Himmler was not yet finished. He summoned a prisoner into a waiting room. The young man shuffled in with his face lowered, although when he drew nearer to the Reichsführer he lifted it. The prisoner wore a pink star pinned to his breast. This showed he was imprisoned for homosexuality.

'Sit,' Himmler said nodding to the chair opposite. The emancipated boy sat wincing with pain. A ceiling fan wheeled above them. Himmler shook his head with disgust. 'You're a disgrace, do you know that?'

The boy stared ahead at nothing. Himmler seethed. 'How could you do it to your mother, your father, me?'

The boy said nothing. He lowered his eyes and blinked. Himmler stared at him. 'What would you do if you were me? Do you know how bad this looks? A homosexual nephew! Do you? Of course not. The only person you've ever loved is yourself.'

The boy's lips trembled and he blinked rapidly. He sat with his gaunt arms folded across his hollow chest. The hunch blades of his shoulders protruding like shark fins. His ribs visible where the shirt was unbuttoned.

'Get out.' Himmler said and the boy rose and tottered out of the room not lifting his head. A guard was there to meet him at the door. He seized the boy's arm and led him away. A general entered, turned his head to glance at the boy, and then shut the door. He walked over to the chair where the boy had sat and sank into it. 'What shall we do with him, Herr Reichsführer?'

'Kill him.'

Before departing, Himmler stopped at the herb garden that he was particularly proud of. Some of the new medicinal supplies had already grown up to his thighs. He lowered himself on one knee and plucked the chilli. 'This contains capsaicin,' he told his driver Sturmbannführer, holding the plant proudly aloft while he sniffed it. 'It relieves muscular pain. A present to the good doctor, Kersten.'

Kersten was called into the Reichsführer's office. Himmler sounded well and so Kersten had a suspicion he was summoned not for therapy, but for something else. He found Himmler at his desk. He seemed agitated. Kersten could tell by the way Himmler pushed his spectacles up and down his nose.

'You must liquidate your house The Hague in Holland. This is your home now. With me. You have ten days to get your affairs in order.'

Kersten flew to Holland to farewell his beloved home. He thought about his meeting with Kivimaki. He wanted to help but he didn't know how. Yet he would not let an opportunity like this slip without trying to wield the influence he may have.

A stocky hand reached into the darkness and flicked on a light switch. Kersten stood silently in the lounge room. It was good to be finally free from his wearisome travels, the transient streets and hordes of anonymous faces.

Kersten turned the key and entered. The large house with all its master paintings mounted on the plaster walls seemed familiar as an old friend one is happy to see. He had barely entered than he rang some close friends to come visit him. Only old Bignall refused to come for he said he was feeling ill. Kersten said he would miss the auctioneer and antiquarian who he had thanked for the oil paintings on these walls that he would have to farewell. While Kersten waited for his guests, he sat back in his pincushion chair and drank hot chocolate dunked with teaspoons of sugar. Soon he heard a knock at his door. He found two old patients waiting for him.

'Come in.' Kersten said waving them in.

'We brought wine,' one said holding up a bottle of Red.

'I'll get glasses.' Kersten smiled slapping both men on the back as he led him through the house. Soon they were joined by several others; some ex patients, some art lovers Kersten had met years ago. The group sat around the lounge room handing around the bottles of wine telling stories about the SS. Kersten listened without interrupting. He only told them not to spare any detail. The men revealed how the Gestapo arrested people for no reason, and beat them or stuck electrical cords to their genitalia. Many of their friends had been deported to concentration while others had been slaughtered. Kersten's closes friend, Rustger, informed Kersten how the Gestapo tied the women's hands behind their back and led them to the scaffold where they waited for the sound of the grating iron. Many of these details, Kersten had heard before. Others, he hadn't. He was touched by all he heard.

When the brass grandfather clocked in the midnight, many guests rose gingerly and said it was getting late. Only Kersten's closest friends remained. Rustger had gone silent from speaking of the brutal tales he could not understand. His eyes were drawn. He looked exhausted. Face pale as white paper. Kersten leant close into his circle of friends who watched him curiously.

'I believe I've come to have influence over Himmler. I know how stress and imagination affect our health. Excitement, fear, worry, overwork and depression constantly affect the vaso-motor function of our vessels and therefore our circulation, digestion and our internal secretion. These mental disturbances manifest in the body through nerves. Nerves require oxygen, nourishment and the dispersal of unwanted blood. That is where these come in…'

Kersten held up his strong, short hands. 'Not so many doctors know this. Patients pass through the hands of medical experts who make them feel that they are only feigning illness. I not only free them from this stigma, but cure them. This inspires their confidence.'

Rustger knew very well how important health was. The Ancient Greeks philosophised how man was nothing without it and called it the most vital necessity.   Kersten continued. 'You must write my office and tell me everything you can find out: imprisonments for no reason, theft and unfair punishments.'

'But how do we send them.' Rustger asked holding his hands out in despair.

'Send them to Military Postal Sector No. 35360. I guarantee these letters will remain secret.'

Rustger frowned. 'But how do you know that address is safe?'

Kersten smiled wryly. 'It's Himmler's.'

CHAPTER 11

Four days passed. On each day Kersten fronted the SS Headquarters or Hauptamt as requested. On the fifth day, Kersten answered a call from Rustger who sounded short of breath like he was drowning.

'What is it, Rustger?'

'They've arrested old man Bignell.'

Kersten mounted the steps to Bignell's apartment with cane in hand. He found police guarding the entrance. The sentinel standing before him sunk deep into a hard SS helmet nodded at Kersten who smiled ironically and returned down the stairs, silent as a stone. He paused once grasping the bannister to take a breath. He decided to visit chief, Hans Albin Rauter at once. He would not wait for his anger to ebb. Kersten would strike while he was brave with rage. While he trudged down the stairs he remembered the promise he made to the Finnish Embassy and to his friends' only days before. He was now more than a therapist. He was an assistant to justice. A conspirer with the devil.

Rauter, who hated Kersten as much as any SS man was angry to see Kersten standing before him, sweating and trembling with outrage. As always, Rauter was immaculately dressed in his pressed uniform. His face hard and masculine. Pompous like all the SS. He studied Kersten silently.

'Free my friend, Bignell. He's innocent. You're men must have mistaken.'

'They were only acting on orders. My orders. He's communicating with London and will be punished.'

'Free him.' Kersten said raising his voice that sounded no longer his own. But his anger meant nothing to Rauter. Kersten leant forward on Rauter's desk. 'You have a telephone.'

'Of course.'

'Get me Himmler in Berlin.'

Rauter laughed with disbelief.

'That's impossible. Even for me.'

'Try it anyway, we shall see.'

It was too late for Kersten to turn back. He seized the phone from Rauter's desk. When Himmler finally answered, Kersten realised the line he had crossed, and for a moment he paused. He was trying to be clever and would be punished for it. What form it would take defeated Kersten's imagination.

Rauter continued staring with his heavy lidded eyes at Kersten. He seemed stunned as Kersten at this boldness.

'One of my best friends has been arrested. I guarantee his innocence. Please do me a favour, Reichsführer, and release him.'

Himmler seemed little interested. 'When are you coming back?'

Kersten knew Himmler was in pain. His request would be the easier for it.

'I'm not done yet. If my friend is arrested, I will be in no shape to help anyone, not even you.'

'Where are you?'

'Rauter's office.'

'Put him on.'

My hand is not shaking, Kersten thought, as the receiver left his fingers.

Rauter nodded. 'Very good, Reichsführer! At once, Reichsführer.'

Kersten seized the phone. Sweat ran into his eyes and his heart galloped. He could be arrested right there for causing trouble. This time he had gone too far. He thought about his family. What would they do if something happened to him? Himmler sounded calm.

'I trust you and have freed your friend. But you must come back quickly.'

'Thank you, Reichsführer. Thank you.'

The phone went dead.

CHAPTER 12

A fine Berlin day. Kersten stood over Himmler while massaging him.

'Why do you hate Jews so much?' Kersten asked. 'They provide industry, and they have fought beside our soldiers for this very soil. Some have died defending Germany.'

'The Jews work for their own community. They do not give back to the community but only use their resources to drain others and to build their Empire. Like a vampire that milks the world's blood. As for those who gave their lives for others, they are the exception. They are outcasts from their own kind. And their kin even find uses for these who wander from the circle. They make great spies, willing or not.'

'Could we not benefit with such realistic characteristics?'

'Indeed, yes. The German forgets the fatherland all too quickly when he's abroad.'

Himmler paused. 'The Jewish Empire gained its working capital and its material substance out of the bankruptcy of national character. That is its strength. The Jew is neither better nor worse than any other people. But each must be bounded by its own form of existence and culture. Otherwise there can only be a struggle of life and death. Do we germanise the Jews? No, but they turn us into Jews.'

The room fell silent. Himmler continued: 'It disgusts me when I see a Jew strolling on the Bavarian mountains in Lederhosen. I don't go about in a caftan and ringlets!'

Kersten smiled at the thought.

'The so- called German Jew doesn't work for Germany, but only for Jews. Das Judenreich comes before all others, draining the world of its materials, strength, riches. They influence other races to transfer everything to themselves.'

'I should remind you,' Kersten began, 'that The Elders of Zion supported a Jewish global conspiracy that people proved a fraud.'

'Only after Jewish bribery made experts say otherwise. Listen Kersten, what binds man is not love but the enemies he shares.'

Kersten heard his voice firm with growing confidence. 'About those experts. You could rip the carpet from under anyone's feet if you wanted to. What if someone viewed Nationalist Socialism from that historical point of view?'

Himmler said nothing. But Kersten thought he could hear the wheels turning in his patient's mind.

The next time Himmler called Kersten to his office it was to berate him.

'Didn't I order you to liquidate your Hague estate?'

'Yes, but my mission was called short. Remember?

'Well, prepare your things. We're leaving tomorrow.'

On June '44 Kersten once more found himself aboard Himmler's carriage that dragged him across the countryside where they stopped at several headquarters. The camps in the forest were often crude. One had a theatre but the seats were too narrow for Kersten's rump that spread awkwardly over it. The chair did not survive and fell dead in a heap of splinters. Kersten raised this one evening with Himmler who he found reading in his bunker.

'You shouldn't read so much, Herr Himmler. Your eyelids are turning red.'

The next day, as Himmler promised, Kersten found an exclusive leather chair in the theatre waiting for him. But his pain still did not cease. He missed his two sons and wife. At night he lay listening to the muted roar of Russian planes, lit up and distant, gliding through the branches of an oak tree outside his window. One morning, just after midnight, he put his face to this window when the alarm wailed. He watched Himmler fleeing to his shelter, his balding head shining in the moonlight like a wet stone, his long nightshirt flapping at his gaunt ankles, as though he were fleeing from a bed that had caught on fire.

CHAPTER 13

Germany entered Russia and their successes at first followed them. Operation Barbarossa had been in the pipeline for years. Germany began with an air assault on Russia's inferior but important air force. The Soviets lost a quarter of it in a single day. One week into the invasion and 150,000 Soviet soldiers were dead or wounded. The Russian high command was like a beast cut in twain, and gave contradictory orders while Germany advanced. Kiev fell and with it 60,000 Soviet officers who surrendered, dragging their lowered, filthy heads from the trench like a band of walking dead. As the Nazis pounded Moscow, Stalin organised a 'getaway' team and contemplated a peace plan.

For now at least it seemed Hitler would have his slave of Slavs, or 'rabbit families' as he called them, his untermensche, who were barely even adequate for this task.

Himmler's pain grew with his responsibilities. It was his task to Germanise Poland and France. Russia would become the next colony under the Reich's draconian hammer. The volksdeutsche of France and Luxembourg alone were headaches enough, for many wanted to stay citizens of their former countries. The frustration was for Himmler, as it was for Hitler, unbearable. The German eagle had spread its wings to encompass all of Western Europe save Britain, which along with Russia and America remained the Führer's most dangerous foes.

Kersten noticed his boss's growing worries that he voiced to his 'Little Buddha', Kersten. But as he did so his voice remained flat and dull as his eyes. They were inside Himmler's office. The room had an uncomfortable emptiness to it, as though Himmler was hiding someone from sight in a secret cavity. Unlike the party members surrounding him, Himmler could talk with Kersten on a simply human level.

'I will tell you everything,' he told Kersten. 'You are my only friend. After we took France we asked England for peace. But the Jews who run the country refused.' Himmler paused to shake his lowered head. 'There will be no peace on earth as long as they are in power, that's to say, as long as they exist. The Führer has told us to liquidate them.'

'Liquidate?'

'Kill the entire race.'

Kersten's eyes widened. 'You cannot do it. History will never forgive you. You will become the world's biggest butcher.'

Himmler spoke without looking at Kersten. 'I begged him not to assign me this mission. He roared at me, 'how do you betray me when I have made you everything you are.'

For a long time no one spoke. Himmler, at last, broke this solemn silence.

'The Führer is always right.'

The Russian endlosung, the liquidation Himmler revealed to Kersten, soon begun. The soldiers rounded up women, children and men who choked on their sobs as they removed their clothes and edged to the lip of a trench, naked. There they saw those shot before them. They climbed into the dirt where an officer walked them to a space where an executioner put bullets in the back of their necks. Large black holes would appear in the Jews' temples and they would fall in strange, twisted positions. Otherwise the soldiers would simply fire their machine guns at row after row of prisoners who would plunge into the gullets of the ditches onto warm bodies below, some of them still jerking. Even when these pits were covered with dirt the blood would gush out like a geyser. As gun smoke wafted about the SS would go among the dead like black vultures in fog, stepping over heads, waving the black birds away with their caps as they wrenched gold fillings from gaping mouths. Some tossed infants in the air and shot them for target practice.

Long after the firing ceased moans could be heard from the ditch. A few survivors managed to claw themselves out at nightfall but they never escaped far. SS soon hunted them out of their holes and clubbed them to death or burnt them alive in barns and synagogues. The flames rose to such heights that it appeared the woods were on fire. The soldiers watched the blazes from afar grinning all the while, some of them drinking themselves to craziness. Like entities from an older age. Wrapped in satanic black leather trench coats. Others blew pipes watching flames bright as blood. Flames that rose like devil horns. Death without tears.

The fighters committed bodies of whole families on the vast open air pyres and the stench of burning flesh wafted for miles to the town folk who spoke about 'Jew burning'. The SS pounded the stairways with their boots in the villages, and shot down doors. They seized babies from their wailing mothers' and they swung them against brick walls or held them aloft over balconies before dropping them to the cement where their tiny skulls would smash like eggshells. In one building a Jewish boy hid in the oven. When he pulled himself out his family was gone. Bonfires raged about down below in the streets the boy was too afraid to see let alone walk. The flames hissed and roared, rising angrily like forked serpent tongues. With them came the victims' cries. The boy crouched with his heels dug in the floor as he played his violin, trying to drown a mother's screams in the neighbourhood.

CHAPTER 14

Kersten had heard of the concentration camp only twelve miles from his country home. Many farmers who lived nearby were using Jehovah Witnesses for labor on their properties. Hitler prosecuted these people who refused to worship him and fight. Kersten, who had known people of this faith in the past, asked Himmler if he could have some workers sent to him. He asked in the middle of a session when he knew the chief was especially relaxed and susceptible.

'How many would you like, Herr Kersten.'

'What about 8, 15 women?'

'I'll spare you ten.'

'Thank you, Reichsführer. You're very kind.'

The number soon grew to include several men. The Kerstens treated the workers well. On one crisp evening, Kersten summoned them to a long table in his backyard. Irmgard and her helpers had cooked a pot of stew. Some of the workers were still dirty from their work in the fields and around the yard. At the head of the table sat Kersten beaming around at the Witnesses with his fleshy, amiable face.

'Let's eat,' he said sinking a fork into his mouth. Everyone solemnly bowed their heads into their bowls and ate while the sun sunk behind them.

After dinner everyone felt relaxed and Kersten took the opportunity to speak what had long been on his mind. 'You must tell me how they treated you at the camps.'

No one said anything. Finally, a woman at the end of the table cleared her throat. 'It's terrible.' Katja said. 'We live in filth. Even the bread and soup they give us is filthy. It's hell. We sleep on harden wooden bunks in dirty clothes. They beat us with whips. They make us sing their stupid songs while saluting. Sometimes they force us to stand in one spot for an entire day, no matter how cold or hot it is. They force us to push full wheelbarrows with our necks while crawling on our hands and knees while they kick and beat us.'

'Has anyone died?' Kersten asked mournfully. An old man by the name of Fritz spoke. 'I heard Germans suffocated two people in a locked closet.'

The young woman at the head of the table rose from her chair, her eyes welling. She walked over to Kersten and threw her arms around his broad, bulky shoulders and sobbed into them.

'Thank you Doctor, thank you.'

Kersten stroked her hair. He lowered his head grimly as though he were praying.

CHAPTER 15

Himmler's Ukraine bunker was in Zhitomir, an old Russian barrack, surrounded by wall of spikes. Trucks would roar up and down the dirt roads day and night. Men in black trench coats came and went bearing suitcases. Headlights drifted in the blackness like halos. Sometimes, Kersten heard birds singing. He wished for them to flee and never to return. Here he took a chance to investigate the Jehovah claims with Himmler. Kersten told Himmler a lie: he said he had seen photographs from journalists who had since fled to their native Switzerland. These pictures showed SS torturing prisoners. Kersten spoke about this when he was half way through the therapy, when Himmler was sighing with relief as his pain ebbed.

'Is it true?'

'You don't understand.' Himmler replied. 'You're not a Nazi. A thousand years from now people will know the real Germans who fought the Jews and they will admire these pictures and will be rightfully grateful to Adolf Hitler for all eternity.'

Kersten pondered his words carefully. Himmler spoke. 'To execute thousands of people and remain decent, that is what has and will continue to toughen us. Our page in history will be the most glorious.'

'That's not being a soldier. It's being an executioner.'

'Wrong. These men in camp are soldiers. Only failed ones.'

Himmler paused before explaining. 'The army brings the soldier before the committee that hears his crime. He can be punished or sent to a camp. If he chooses the latter his superior asks him if he would like to torture someone to death. If he refuses he must return to his punishment. Usually, the soldier stays. He kills the first person reluctantly. The second time it's easier. He gets a taste for it, and he even boasts of his deeds. Before he has chance to talk we liquidate and replace him.'

'You made this system?'

'No. The Führer's genius extends even to the smallest details.'

'And the tortures?'

'How could I question the greatest mind that ever been? But I've never hurt anyone, nor could I.'

Kersten pondered. 'If Hitler asked you to kill your wife and family would you do so?'

'Without thinking, yes.'

Kersten finished the treatment. 'History will remember you as the greatest murderer of all time.'

'No. I am merely following the orders of a genius. That is important'

Kersten's face looked pale with anger. He glared at Himmler, but spoke gently. 'You're a spiritual man, Herr Himmler. Are you not frightened of how heaven will judge your deeds?'

Himmler gave a museful sigh. 'It may be more pleasant to concern myself with flowerbeds than political dust heaps, but flowers cannot thrive unless these things are seen to.'

Kersten lowered his head. Himmler's voice sounded distant to him. Like a dream receding as you claw yourself from the grave of sleep.

'Extermination is a messy business.' Himmler said. 'Innocent people are too stupid to understand its necessity. I'm aware of that.'

CHAPTER 16

Life in Berlin was serene and quiet. The Kerstens understood they were Germany's hostages. But they lived comfortably and Himmler paid Kersten well. The German people, fanatical and patriotic though they were, did not want war. Kersten even heard whispers that Hitler did not desire it. Yet England would not stand aside. Now the German war machine was spreading its tentacles across Europe and towards their arch enemies: the Russian's Bolsheviks. More than once Hitler had openly denounced these guardians of international Jewry. The man who took acting classes and trained for hours in front of mirrors seduced his people, waving his hand triumphantly aloft while his blue eyes gazed down like a God upon the jostling, teary eyed crowd from his podium. What he said may have been lies but they were more awe inspiring to Germany than any truths. Yet not all of these citizens benefited from Nazi dictatorship. One day, Kersten's industrialist friend Rosterg, pulled Kersten aside at a dinner party. He was tall, greying but normally impeccable in his suits with a glowing complexion. But today Kersten found him pale and preoccupied as he herded Kersten into the kitchen.

'You must help me, Kersten.'

Kersten stared at his friend. 'What do you mean?'

'The German police have arrested my foreman. He's a good friend. He's done nothing wrong besides being a Social democrat. He doesn't deserve to be sent to a concentration camp. I was wondering if you could give a good word for him.'

Kersten watched his friend so helpless standing before him, throwing brandy down his throat as though it were water. Kersten's eye finally flashed, as though he has seen something that only he could see. Rosterg smiled. 'You're going to help me, aren't you?'

'We shall see.'

Kersten squeezed his friend's shoulder sympathetically. But for now he would promise nothing.

The session ended, as usual, with Himmler's satisfaction. The war gave the SS leader more burdens and responsibilities than his health could bear. He also had Heydrich breathing down his throat, ready to take over his job if he made mistakes. These troubles brought out the Reichsführer's self-pity. Kersten saw it all too well. On the outside Himmler was a strong, masculine nation socialist. But Kersten had found Himmler's fragility, his uncertainty, his weakness. Himmler needed Kersten more than ever.

Today, Kersten removed a note from his wallet. The paper rustled in his shaking hands as he unfolded it in the silence. There was no turning back from what he was about to do. Who knew where this would end.

'This is my fee, Reichsführer, this man's freedom.'

Himmler seized the note, his flabby muscles jostling in the dimness. He held the paper below his eyes. A long silence passed between them. He studied Kersten, who stood serenely, his powerful chest stretched out, his rosy face and blue eyes smiling.

'Since it is you asking, I shall of course grant it.'

Kersten almost collapsed. Himmler turned his head towards the adjoining room. 'Brandt, I wish to release a gentleman. Our good doctor wishes it.'

Kersten could not believe it. He had stolen a life.

~

The more the war raged on the worse Himmler's pains became and the more he depended on his doctor who seemed to accompany him everywhere. Kersten was given access to Himmler's direct international landline, the only one beside Hitler's in Germany. He received uncensored mail in Himmler's mailbox that only he and Brandt could access. But he had advised his friends long before to deliver these letters in a special way.

'And how is that?' Rosterg asked. They were sitting in Kersten's back garden overlooking the brave mountains that shadowed the valley. The sun was sinking and birds were puffing out their chests and crying sharply. *What harsh noises they scream from their tiny bodies*, Kersten noticed. He turned to Rosterg who raised his cup and saucer to his lips. He examined the doctor from over the rim of the cup that he lifted to his mouth.

'They must deliver their envelopes smelling of perfume.'

Rosterg gave a puzzled laugh. 'But why, Felix?'

Kersten smiled. 'So I can tell Himmler they are love letters from my girlfriends in Holland.'

Rosterg laughed.

'It's true,' Kersten said. 'He loves to hear about my imaginary girlfriends. He lives through me, I think. I imagine deep down he still aspires to be the Aryan stud instead of the Baltic weakling he knows himself to be. Do you know he holds gymnastic classes for his staff?'

'Nooo…'

'I watched one once. Himmler, being the old fashioned conservative he is at heart, came to his class in a full length body stocking. He did star jumps, but had to stop when he went green after only a few minutes. His strength is no better than his endurance. He couldn't do a single chin up.'

Rosterg shook his head.

'His trunk stretching has to be seen to be believed.

43

CHAPTER 17

A booming voice echoed through the wooden stable barrack. 'Get up' it said. Martine raised her head. The moon shone blue through the window. 'Outside now.' The guard yelled swinging his rifle, foaming like a dog and the women ambled outside. It was three in the morning and so cold they shivered in their rags, their eyes blinking in their hollow sockets, and they stood and stood until an hour passed whereupon a guard with a square head loped out to meet them wrapped in a fur coat bearing under his arm a roll that he called names from, many of whom wanted it simply all to end. His voice reached their exhausted ears like a distant noise. A muted rumbling. One girl collapsed but no one dared help her. A fresh faced soldier stood over her and gave her his hand and when she took it he hit her so hard her nose caved in and so much blood gushed from it into her mouth she gurgled and vomited over herself. An older man came over and patted the young man's back to congratulate him while another squatted on his heels like an owl over the moaning victim, shoving a camera in her face that made a sensuous puff.

Later that day Martine was walking back to the barracks after work when she saw a friend of hers, a pretty girl, Corinne making eyes to an SS officer who had just emerged from one of the barracks. Following him was his wife, a beautiful blonde who saw the amorous exchange. At once, the blonde's face stiffened. She led her husband angrily by his arm towards their car. Corinne lowered her head and walked on.

Martine squeezed her friend's arm and dragged her behind a wall. 'What do you think you're doing?'

Corinne frowned. She had very blue eyes, long black hair and alabaster skin.

'He does me favours. He gives me wine, chocolate, cigarettes. Sometimes, we even dance. I think we may be falling in love.'

'You silly girl. Just listen to yourself. Look around at where we are.'

'Exactly. He makes me feel human again. Do you remember what that's like? Maybe you don't. That is why you don't understand.'

Corinne stormed away stiffly, her ragged shoes splashing in the muddy puddles. Martine followed her with her eyes. She saw the handsome officer with the blond wife walking towards her. He looked pale and livid. For now he did nothing. But even as he passed her he stared at Corinne from under the shelter of his skull and cross bones hat. This would be not the end of it. Martine knew that. She turned away. *This world is like no other*, she realised. No one could have been prepared to live in such an unnatural place.

The next day Martine shuffled off early to work with the others. She was angry with Corinne. Not just angry because she bragged, although she was angry at that too. It had taken Martine a lot of time and discipline to forget about the outside world. When Martine first arrived she used to reconstruct her old life in her imagination, but this meant she had to reconstruct its loss as well. To experience something once is often more than enough. But to have memory so we can relive it endlessly is one of God's cruelest jokes.

The sun had not yet risen. Their breaths steamed in the cold. Martine saw a pair of legs stretched out behind a wall. She neared closer and saw a puddle of blood beneath them. Corinne's overalls had been ripped open with a knife, and someone had removed her butchered breast. It lay beside her like a strange motif. Martine walked on.

Corinne was her friend. But Martine did not cry. No one here did anymore. Everyone had to live for themselves. *She is dead, I am alive. The world is simple and brutal. All that matters no longer matters behind the wires.*

They were all rats on a wheel. The Nazis had turned them into the rodents they had proclaimed them to be. Martine was too tired for fear. She simply breathed and she barely seemed aware of that. Her feet moved so she walked. And when she thought, she tried to think of nothing.

CHAPTER 18

The letters that fed through Kersten's hands made them tremble. He waited until he reached his home where he could read them in private. He selected the worse and burnt the others in his garden. While these letters smouldered in flames he imagined families being rounded up in their homes by military police and marshalled through the door into waiting SS trucks that roared away in the night through narrow winding streets that seemed to embody the crazy mind of this new world. He wondered of the camps where the police took them, the tortures, the labour they endured, and the lonely cages where they thought of death with their knees drawn up under blankets that smelt of urine or with their heads hung between their knees. Kersten always had reservations about collecting these letters. Yet when he read them his compassion defeated his fear, until he stood face to face with something divine and transcendent. After those moments, he knew he had to act, no matter what.

Having burned the letters, Kersten kept their names. While he massaged Himmler's back he asked the Reichsführer to free more people. By now Kersten had a plan. He asked for lives when Himmler was in the deepest throes of agony. Otherwise, he appealed to Himmler's vanity.

'Release them. People will remember you for years to come. You will be the equal of Henry the Fowler. But like these men your fame will rest not on courage and force alone, but on your generosity.'

'My dear, Kersten. You are my only friend, my Buddha, the only one who both understands and helps me.'

And so it was Himmler signed the paper that freed prisoners, and like the humble, self- effacing servant he was Brandt would scurry off with the list of people's lives in his hands. One morning he returned to his office with a letter that bore the name of a young French woman, a simple primary school teacher, but a dangerous traitor to the Nazis, nevertheless.

The women shuffled out of their huts, lifted their eyes and looked at the sky for the last time. The clouds looked so low in places they seemed to be falling. All the women so thin. Little more than bones. It hurt them even to walk. Eyes bloated in their dull sockets. No life in them. The Nazis had beaten that out of them long ago.

What a thing it is to die, Martine thought. *What does one compare it to?* The snow sloshed beneath their unkempt shoes and crunched in their ears. It's whiteness before them stretched far as they could see.

The SS men with their skull embroidered jackets and caps, were waiting for them in the clearing, their rifles at rest by their sides. How many times had Martine seen these men knock women down with the butts of these weapons? They drank, smoked and sang late into the night, and all the staff was fucking each other. It was all a party for them.

While the women marched to their deaths, huddled together like a flock of geese, the wind whistled in their ears and scalded their eyes. It drove a curtain of snow across the slopes like an invisible hand, covering their solemn, lowered faces in mist. Some of the flying ice particles snared itself on the barbed wire fence that ran along the camp. The last thing Martine would see would be those wire thorns, the miles of snow weighing the world down and the faceless men shooting her, whom she wanted to forget most of all.

Guards shoved the women into a line. Teeth chattered. The prisoners blinked their eyelashes thatched with snow. The SS, shrouded behind their caps, watched them. Such young men. The wind smelt like ice. Everything was grey. The women trembled and sobbed. Cold and lonely. A girl went to seize her friend's hand but the guard saw it and he knocked their fingers apart.

The strange sky dropped tiny pebbles of rain. The executioners raised their rifles, leant their weapons into the hollows of their shoulders and cocked them. This was done in one synchronous motion. The women stood mute as stone. Martine felt rain in her hair, running down her nose.

Silence. Martine closed her eyes. Or at least she thought she did. She could not be sure. Then a voice called. 'Warten, warten!'

Martine turned her head. A stocky man came crunching through the snow holding up his gloved hand. His face looked flushed from exertion. The SS lowered their rifles. Not even the soldiers knew what was happening.

The fat man stood with the executioners who nodded as they listened. The fat man turned around and studied the pitiful prisoners, holding the letter in his hands. 'Prisoner 1023, step forward,' he said. A girl two people up from Martine took one footstep.

'No.' the fat man retorted holding the note closer to his eyes. 'Prisoner 1033. Step forward.'

Martine obliged. Her number was her name now. She had no other. She wondered what would happen to her. Perhaps one of the doctors wanted to use her in their experiments.

The squat officer with the bull neck waved her over to him. His jaw moved down. "Come' he said, and he met her half way and studied her face up close. He breathed deeply. He pulled up her left sleeve. 'You're a very lucky girl. Someone in high places likes you.'

Then with a nod to the left. 'Go back to quarters. Someone is waiting there to escort you home.'

Martine almost fainted. She turned around and trudged through the slush, the wind rearing behind her where she heard the explosion of rifles that echoed long through the stillness. Then nothing.

CHAPTER 19

Kersten awoke when he heard someone ringing his doorbell at his Berlin apartment. He opened one red eye. His bedside clock read 6.00 am. When Kersten opened his door he found two SS men. The older of the two spoke in a flat voice. 'Herr Felix Kersten, you are under arrest.'

~

Himmler removed the phone from his phone cheek. Without looking at Kersten he spoke.

'You were arrested for treating Jews.' He put the receiver back to his ear. 'I forbid anyone to interfere with Dr. Kersten for any reason whatsoever. This is an order. The doctor is responsible to me and me alone.'

Himmler slammed down the phone so hard Kersten swore he felt the Reichsführer's desk tremble. When Himmler looked up he was pale, and his spectacles moved up and down.

'You cannot be my doctor and treat Jews. They are lower than animals.'

'The Jew is as well made as any other man. Besides, I am not German, remember.'

~

At No.8 Prinz Albrecht-Strasse the most seemingly German of them all was also the most fearsome: Reinhard Heydrich. Even Hitler called him the 'man with the iron heart.' He was an excellent fencer, and he took this sport so seriously that he did not execute the umpires who judged against him in tournaments.

When the Gestapo rolled into Poland, Heydrich immediately liquidated threats to national security. At the top of his list was a group of girl scouts aged between twelve and sixteen who were lined up against a wall and shot along with the priest who read them their rites. Their blood was left for the flies, drying in the market square where it turned black.

So Heydrich acquired his nickname of Blonde Beast.

The night after his first bloody crusade Reinhard celebrated by playing his violin to his beautiful mistress who sat curled up in his bed, her firm breasts exposed beneath her lace gown, her cunt shining between her moist thighs like a pearl in the moonlight. He played it so sensitively that he wept. The sweet, melancholy strains of music also carried his lover away, until a smile rose to her blood red lips and her eyes also filled with tears.

Unlike Himmler, Reinhard embodied the Aryan ideal of the tall, blonde, blue eyed brute, although Himmler had told Kersten that Heydrich lived with rumours that he belonged to Jewish ancestry. These accusations had dogged him from his schooldays when the children called him Goat for his falsetto voice. He certainly had the long nose of a Jew, Kersten observed, and he used this nose to sniff out trouble. Heydrich also had big ears that like antennas heard everything. These skills came naturally to him, although he had learnt them only after he bluffed himself into his job after failing in the navy. By then even Hitler knew about the Jewish rumours. So Heydrich had to prove his worth. Himmler told Kersten that Heydrich exceeded himself to make up for his biological shortcomings that enflamed him with guilt.

Did Hitler know the truth, Kersten thought? Of course he did. Hitler was perverse. He once lost his temper and hurled himself onto a carpet so he could chew it. He was just the type to enjoy the delicious irony of employing a man with Jewish blood to execute the final solution.

'You let him stay. Even when you knew-'

'The Führer knows. Heydrich isn't the first with Jewish blood to be given Aryan status.'

'Others have come before...'

Himmler's voices quieten although they were alone in his office.

'Emil Maurice was with Hitler from the beginning. He was the Führer's head bodyguard and a co-founder of the SS. In 35 they uncovered his Jewish heritage and gave him Aryan status. The Jewish nightclub magician Erik Jan Hanussen would have been given the status had he survived.'

'I'm not familiar with him.'

'He was a telepath who befriended Hitler long ago. He told the Führer to make speeches at night when listeners' psychological resistance waned. He taught Hitler to gesture, time and inflect.'

'To act...'

'And self-confidence.'

'What happen to this sorcerer?'

'He was murdered in 1933. After days of heavy rain a farmer found a foot sticking out of the earth. It belonged to the magician. Hitler wanted to kill the Nazis' responsible: Helldorf and Ernst. Josef Goebbels convinced the Führer to spare Helldorf. But Ernst was later shot dead by my SS. Their motives remained unclear. Even to me.'

CHAPTER 20

Of late, Heydrich, with usual efficiency, had created a high class brothel that doubled as a goldmine of information. He had visited the Salon Kitty only a few times, and during some of those calls he enjoyed the whores. Unlike so many Nazi buildings, the Saloon wasn't imposing, which was just as well. The cream building had a softer elegance to it, which obviously made the patrons- diplomats mostly-feel at home. This was Heydrich's intention. While the important guests fucked the prostitutes, five operators hunched over speakers in the murky basement made transcripts of all they heard from microphones hiding behind paintings, under armchairs, inside lamps and on top of wardrobes. The microphones and cameras never ceased. The whores, twenty of Berlin's best, had been arrested then trained to manipulate information from diplomats and military leaders. At first the girls feared the Gestapo. But Heydrich's knowledge transcended the usual and every day. He gave the honey pots chewing gum. 'We can't have you crying,' he said. "If you ever feel the urge, chew.' They nodded their pretty heads. Chomp, chomp. 'Yes sir!'

So far the SS had gleaned little from the pillow talk, besides discovering that their favourite customer, the Italian statesman Ciano, a friend of that sly bastard Felix Kersten, had ranted his disgust and hatred for Hitler which made everyone laugh.

Heydrich met Officer Ernst Kaltenbrunner in a back room downstairs. The second in charge was late. He found the 6 foot 7 Ernst waiting for him with a Brandy married to his hand. By all appearances, Heydrich's guest had had enjoyed his visit. His collar was undone and his glazed eyes looked far away. Ernst was not exactly Heydrich's friend. Reinhard didn't have those. He could not sacrifice his lust for glory with relationships. But Ernst and he did understand each other.

The two towering Nazis greeted each other not with a Nazi salute, but with a friendly handshake. Heydrich apologised for his tardiness and sat opposite his Austrian guest who smiled with a scarred face that was severely pitted. Reinhardt removed his cap and placed it before him on the wooden table while Ernst finished his glass.

Kitty Schmidt, a handsome madam from Vienna with dark hair wafted in bearing two fresh glasses that she placed on the table. She smiled and exited silently.

'How is der Himmler?' Ernst asked.

'He talks not like a normal man, but like a moraliser or a philosopher. I think he comes from another planet.'

Ernst smiled as though he understood something that escaped even Heydrich's cold and superior intelligence. 'Oppression is the essence of power. He told me that once. Don't tell him that I use that quote as my own every time opportunity presents.'

Ernst lifted his glass, his eyes smiling at Heydrich over its rim. When he slammed down the empty cup he drew a long, satisfied sigh putting his palms face down on each knee.

'He's favourite slogan, however says: Never forget. We are the knightly order. Did you know he even has a skull on his hanky? That is dedication for you. And maybe that explains why he rose from Nazi member 42,404 to chief of Gestapo. Not bad for a chicken farmer.'

Ernst paused abruptly, smiling at his resourcefulness. Then he filled his glass and topped up Heydrich who drank, before removing a cigarette from a gold case in his jacket that he lit with a zippo lighter that bore skull and cross bones. He leaned back and blew a long satisfying cloud of smoke.

'You love Himmler don't you, Heydrich. You know you're more efficient than him. He lives too much…in a fantasy world that explains his vivid ideas on racial policy. But in the real one, so people tell me, he's…indecisive. He thinks only in black and white.'

Ernst seemed to hide behind the glass that he lifted to his mouth. Heydrich, who had a nose for most things, smelt sex on Ernst. Heydrich was distracted, if only for a moment, by the thought of the fucking he planned on.

'Don't worry, Heydrich. I see your devotion to your master not as a weakness, but as a sign of strength. Himmler loves Germany as much as we do and he is a good, hardworking man with decent character. Now tell me why you brought me here.'

Heydrich sat back, crossing one leg over the other, bouncing his boot while he toyed with its straps.

'I just wanted to show you a good time while you were in town.' Heydrich replied holding out his hands as though to boast.

'Well a bluebird told me Goering likes to visit.' Ernst said tapping the end of his nose. 'He loves the lesbians.'

Heydrich looked at him, laughing and coughing.

'Poor girls.' Ernst continued, not noticing the dismay that suddenly darkened his comrade's face. 'Himmler wouldn't come here, would he? Is he really so conservative. Is that why it took him twenty eight years to get inside a woman?'

But Heinrich was brooding upon other matters that he could not restrain any longer. 'We have a problem.'

Ernst frowned and stiffened, lifting his neck until it was completely erect, stretching far above his drink stained collar. He had no idea what Heydrich was going to say. He made advantage of this brief interruption in conversation to light a cigarette. His fingernails were claw like and black from nicotine. He smiled at Heydrich and the scar on the left of his face curled up turning his smile into a snarl. Heydrich spoke softly and deliberately. 'Kersten.'

'The Reichsmaster's therapist.' Ernst said as though someone had sounded a bell in his head.

'He must be liquidated.' Heydrich muttered through his teeth.

Silence. The two men understood each other perfectly.

'Then who better to dispose of him than 'the Hangman.' Ernst replied raising his schooner that Heydrich, smiling modestly, toasted.

When Ernst lowered his glass, his beaming face paled, and his dwarf hand trembled. Heydrich, who noticed everything, didn't let this escape his scrutiny.

'What's wrong, man?'

'These rooms are bugged. If Himmler knew what we discussed he would have both our heads.'

'Yes, he would. But devices are turned off when I step through these doors.'

Ernst realising he had forgotten himself like a drunk, euphoric lover, breathed a sigh of relief, seized his glass and drank to celebrate his ironic fortune.

CHAPTER 21

Kersten entered Himmler's office, finding the man smiling and speaking into his phone. Sometimes, it seemed the damn thing never ceased ringing.

Kersten moved politely to the chair. He could tell by Himmler's sweet tone the call was a sociable one. Nothing too important it would seem.

'Your boy will grow up and join our SS.' Himmler said with happy pride. 'He will always have a home with us. I assure you of that Mrs. Wolffe. Goodbye to you all.'

Himmler hung up his phone. He looked at Kersten from behind his spectacles.

'Just making sure my flowers arrived to an officer's young wife. She had her first baby last night.'

Kersten smiled. Sometimes when he looked at Himmler he pictured not only a scholar, but a prophet convinced in his vision. At those moments it was easy to understand the power and influence he wielded over so many men. Wherever he cast his shadow, panic quickly followed. He was already taking over the rocket centres on the Baltic where the V rockets were being developed and tested. His ambitions also included taking over the Luftwaffe Research Station. If an outsider saw him, however, they would see only the bespectacled weakling without a chin. Maybe one of the Reichsführer's favourite phrases applied to himself: 'Be more than you appear'.

'Wonderful news. I'll never forget my first...'

Himmler leaned forward, his feminine hands, knotted with vanes, motionless on the desk. 'Is your son like you?'

'Who can tell at that age? He's a good boy.'

Kersten expected Himmler to advise him to prepare his son for work for the Waffen SS or the Gestapo. Often Himmler told him how he loved recruiting men with Saxon ancestry; the thick skulled lot. Proud, pure, and tough was what he called them. He wanted only the flower of races. Himmler wanted to build the ultimate biological army.

He loved to discuss the visions he had for his beloved SS. Light would fill his eyes at such times, like stars passing across the face of the earth. He was as tough on his men as he was kind and fair. He ranted vividly about creating different racial sections, recruiting, of course, and the notion of providing his men only enough wealth to keep them comfortable. Any more than that was an abomination. He said, 'my ambition is to die poor, and I wish the same for my men.' He fell to discussing the Middle Eastern punishment whereby thieves lost their hands. 'If such a thing were

permitted here, many rich people would be walking around minus a limb.'
Maybe he had by accident, overlooked many of his high ranking men who
lived lavishly.

CHAPTER 22

Rudolf Hess was one Nazi Himmler knew would benefit greatly from Kersten's 'magic hands.' The Deputy Führer was a vegetarian, so obsessed with his health and mysticism that he consulted astrologers, fortune tellers and faith healers. He didn't smoke or drink. After a session with Kersten, during which Hess talked about the danger of the Russian campaign, his voice grew dramatic yet earnest. 'I'm going to make history.'

'Why do you say that, Herr Hess?'

'Forget I said anything. Thank you, Kersten. Pass on my best wishes to your family.'

The next time Kersten heard mention of Hess was from Brandt in the secretary's office at SS Headquarters in Berlin. Hess had taken flight in his plane that he had modified with a long-range fuel tank, a radio compass and a modified oxygen system. He avoided capture flying at high speed and low altitude over Scotland. When he reached Eaglesham he ran out of fuel, so he climbed 1,800 feet and parachuted. A ploughman found him struggling from the canopy, as though he was untangling himself from the tentacles of a giant jellyfish. Hess was on a private mission to make peace with Churchill.

'Hess was your patient. You know what Heydrich will say?' Brandt said, as though it were a warning. Kersten watched him fearfully. 'As a friend, I warn you. Heydrich is out to destroy you.'

Kersten removed his favourite brown coat and hat along with his cane in the cloakroom. From there he moseyed into the mess hall where two hundred Nazi agents were seated in their conference. Kersten took a seat in the corner, sitting with his hands folded across his stomach staring into space. Suddenly, Himmler's private guard was hovering over him with rich, cream cakes and strong coffee that Kersten accepted with a smile. He sank his teeth into one of the cakes, relishing its richness, feeling the pleasure seize his blood. He shoveled the sweet so quickly down his throat he covered the top of his mouth with cream that he licked clean along with his white, sugary fingers, making sucking noises. But his peace did not last long. He heard rising voices nearby. One of them belonged to Rauter.

'Those Dutch pigs are in for a surprise, aren't they?'

Heydrich smiled. 'Poland will cool them off. I've just received my deportation plans. You will have the working plans shortly.'

Heydrich continued in a lowered voice Kersten couldn't hear. Kersten put down his half eaten cake. His heart fell out of his chest. He drank the rest of his coffee before shuffling out to a phone that he used to ring

Brandt.

'Can I see you? Alone.'

'My office at six.'

Brandt was more than happy to give Kersten's answers. He removed an envelope sitting on his desk with 'Secret' written across it. Brandt stood close to Kersten. 'This must remain secret.'

Kersten nodded and sank into the chair at Brandt's desk like a deflated balloon. His eyes scrolled the forty-three yellow pages trembling in his hands. Hitler and Boorman had signed them. Brandt leant on the edge of his oak table, silent. The report said it all. The Dutch had to be punished for turning away Hitler's help. Three million men would be sent on foot to the freezing east under the whips and gun butts of German soldiers while the elderly, women and children were sent on ships from Netherlands to Konsogaberg where they would be railed to Lublin, packed together until the air vanished and their lungs ached. Kersten let fall the envelope on the desk, ripped a sheet from one of Brandt's pads and scribbled down what he had read. The whole project would be put in effect on April the 20th, a present to Hitler on his birthday.

Kersten stayed up all night, staring at the ceiling. When he roused at morning he realised he had to tell someone. He came in to the kitchen and handed Elizabeth the note he had written in Brandt's office. While she read it, Kersten paced up and down the room rubbing his forehead, as though he were trying to erase his black thoughts.

'What can I do to stop this?'

'Tell Himmler.'

Kersten kept pacing the length of the room until Elizabeth seized his shoulders.

'You are going to sit in that chair and pull yourself together.'

Kersten did so. 'I will no longer serve these monsters.'

Kersten groaned over his misery. Elizabeth bit her bottom lip. 'You mustn't give up faith. What good are you if you stop treating Himmler? You must continue serving humanity the only way you can.'

'By treating the monsters responsible.'

'You know what William Blake said…'

'What?' Kersten said shaking his head, his jowls trembling.

'Life is a fiction full of contradiction.'

Kersten pressed his hands down into Himmler's flesh.

'What is the exact date of the Dutch deportation?'

'The 20th of April. It's a present for the Führer. I was there with Hitler when news came through of riots in Amsterdam. He went into a rage and said he wanted to resettle all those parasites. How do you know?'

'I overheard Heydrich and Rauter discussing it loudly in the mess hall.'

'Idiots. Thank you for notifying me.'

'As your therapist I advise you not to go ahead with this.'

'Oh…'

'Didn't Hitler ask you to bring the number of SS up to a million before summer that you will have to train, dress and organise? That alone is burden enough. Your work depends on your health. Undertaking two large missions like that will ruin one and hence the other. You work too late as it is.'

'History will enquire not how well Heinrich Himmler slept, but how much he achieved. Besides, we need Germanic blood in Poland. The Dutch will need our protection and help. We will settle Holland and England will lose its best landing ground.'

'Which mission is more important? The SS recruitment project or the deportation?'

Himmler didn't hesitate. 'The SS recruitment without doubt.'

That night Kersten returned home rubbing his hands. Elizabeth who was at the sink preparing dinner turned around as he came through the door.

'I will have him yet.'

'Cease this deportation. For the sake of your health, you must.' Kersten said as his hands sank into Himmler's shoulders. His hands brought relief, but not the answer he wanted. 'I've never seen you so sick. My treatments will do nothing if you do not rest.'

It was true. Himmler was doubled up with cramps. Like a dying insect. Yet he remained a slave to discipline and glory.

'The strain is not yours alone, Reichsführer.' Kersten continued. 'It is no small thing to transport eight million people in the middle of a war. They lack German discipline. Who knows what will happen with them. I warn you as your responsible doctor, this operation is more than your weak body can bear.'

'I cannot. I made a promise to myself. Without honesty a man is nothing.'

On the 18th of April, 1941 Kersten received a call from Himmler who had just returned from visiting Hitler. Kersten expected the worse. He almost cried when Himmler told him the deportation would be postponed until after the war. Kersten hung up the phone. He strolled out to his garden where he took a handful of snowdrops and crocuses that he carried inside to his study where he placed them delicately in front of the picture of the Queen of Holland and Prince Henry that he kept on his writing desk. He sat like a saint before an altar in a heavenly silence that was one of the best he had ever known.

CHAPTER 23

'You look so happy, Reichsführer.' Kersten said as Himmler entered his office for the day's treatment. It was morning, and Himmler looked stronger than he had for weeks. 'My treatment yesterday helped?'

'Did it what, my little Buddha. I slept, as the English say, like a log.'

Kersten took the moment to hand Himmler a document.

'And what is this you're giving me?'

'That Herr Reichsführer, is a memorandum a friend gave me. He believes Russia can never be overcome by a foreign power, for Russians can only be conquered by Russians.'

Himmler glanced through it. 'Interesting.'

~

After supper Himmler received his usual treatment, and he took the opportunity to speak to Kersten about the memorandum.

'Hitler tore it from my hand. 'The victory should be snatched from me' he shouted. I concurred. We alone understand the Russian people and how to deal with them, Kersten.'

'And what do you intend to do with that titan Russia?'

'River Lena will go to England once we resume our friendly relations. The United States will receive the area between the River Lena, Kamschatka and the Sea of Okhotsk.'

'What does Japan get?'

'They have North China, the Philippines and Dutch's colonial possessions.'

Kersten's face dropped. 'It so cruel to take the land away from a Germanic people who worked hard for three hundred years to establish themselves.'

'They should have thought of that before, when the Führer extended his hand. Why should we make sacrifices for a so obstinate people?'

'Please, you know how much this hurts me. Why must you speak so coldly?'

Himmler raised his chin, as Kersten pressed his hands into the Reichsführer's back.

'A statesman must be hard. War is a matter of life and death, and there's no place for sentiment.'

This is his masculine side showing, Kersten thought. *His all or nothing mentality.*

'Perhaps, but it is no crime for a man to open his heart to mercy.'

Himmler laughed. 'You're quiet right. Perhaps one is often too tough.'

Kersten knew this was the time. If he didn't act now it would be too late. He could never know when Himmler's kindness would end. He paused and took a list from his pocket that he read to Himmler who listened silently. The names included 28 Dutchmen, 6 Germans and 4 Norwegians. Himmler snatched the note from Kersten and held it below his nose like he was sniffing it and his small eyes ran over the names, and Kersten thought, what gravity something as simple as a loose paper held. 'Really, I oughtn't to do that.' Himmler replied.

'I know.' Kersten replied. 'But your humane feelings will make you sign a release for these people.'

'For my own sake. But the people don't deserve it.'

Himmler bent over the paper and signed it with a pen Kersten took from the Reichmaster's desk. Himmler threw his legs over the bench and walked over to the phone that he picked up. 'Dr. Brandt.'

Kersten felt his heart leap.

'I have a list of people who must be freed.'

CHAPTER 24

Heydrich was giving Kersten problems, spreading scuttlebutt through headquarters, accusing Kersten of being a spy. So it was little surprise when on the afternoon of the 15th of May 1941 Heydrich suggested to Kersten that they have a little chat. Kersten knew that this could very well be the end of him. Perhaps fortune had already been outrageously kind to him, and he had already used up all he could of it. Every time he opened a new letter and found a request he felt it burn in his hands. How the secret police, who had been so efficient, let this happen, escaped him.

Heydrich studied Kersten for a long time from his horsey face.

'Let's talk now shall we,' Kersten spoke.

Sunlight lit up the curtains of Heydrich's office. He knew Heydrich was angry so he arrived precisely at three as planned. As soon as Kersten stepped across the threshold he heard the doors shut and lock behind him. Kersten sat and waited. The clock arm completed half a circle. He studied the giant wall tapestry embroidered with a huge eagle clasping a swastika with its talons. A photo of Heydrich's wife and children sat on the solid wood desk. Kersten's wristwatch ticked in the silence. Finally, Kersten raised himself half way out of his seat when he heard the lock come undone. Heydrich came in, exceptionally groomed as always. He sat opposite Kersten and took a cigarette from the gold case in his top pocket. He held out the tray to Kersten who sat with his hands stretched across his stomach.

'A cigarette?'

Kersten eyed the cigarettes tentatively from down the end of his nose.

'Don't worry,' Heydrich smiled. 'It's not the drugged type we use to acquire confessions.'

Kersten nodded. 'I don't smoke. But thank you.'

Heydrich leant forward as Kersten remarked about the lovely spring weather. Then he pressed a button below the table. A microphone came alive to record on the gramophone disc that spun silently into action. Kersten smiled humourlessly. 'We should talk at Hartzwalde where we can do so undisturbed. There I can press the button.'

Heydrich released the switch. He leant back and touched his fingers together. 'You know about listening devices then. And politics.'

'Everyone here knows the ropes. I've no political knowledge whatever.'

'So much the worse,' Heydrich replied with a cruel smile, his blue eyes flashing, 'apart from the fact that I don't believe you. But you are treating

61

the Reichsführer, and it happens with great men, when a doctor relieves them from pain, that they regard him as their deliverer and are ready to lend him a sympathetic ear.'

Heydrich paused to ponder. Kersten had to admire Heydrich for his perceptiveness. Himmler's pain compromised his sense of obligation, however strong his self-control.

'When people come and ask you to intervene with the Reichsführer we can help you.'

If Heydrich had such knowledge he would warn Himmler and I will be of no use, Kersten thought trying not to smile ironically. *At least Heydrich had been straight forward. If he found out it won't be only me who is danger, but also those who request my help.*

'You're more than the simple medical man you pretend to be.'

How am I to escape this? I cannot evade his questions forever. And when I tell him of what I've been doing they will execute me. Not even Himmler will be able to save me.

Kersten felt beads of sweat run down his forehead into his eyes. His bottom lip trembled. Heydrich stared at him. Kersten opened his mouth. A spasm in his throat.

'Give me their names.'

This time when Kersten opened his mouth he felt the words surging up from his squirming stomach. But again, his courage deserted him.

Heydrich folded his hands together as though he were praying and leant closer to Kersten across the table. 'I believe you influenced Hess's friendly feelings toward England. Tell me, what was his state of mind while you treated him?'

'It would breach patient doctor confidentiality to discuss that. Besides, he told me nothing about his plans to escape. If he did I would have warned him against it.'

'I'm sorry, but I have to arrest you. I don't believe you. So tell me, what did he tell you, what was his mind set? I don't have to remind you, your family will suffer for your crimes. The Führer is shocked about Hess.'

'He told me nothing.'

'You're lying.'

'I swear on my children's graves, I am not.'

'You influenced Himmler to stop the Dutch deportation plan. You should give me the names of your contacts in Hague. I may be able to protect them.'

Silence.

'Tell me your sources.'

'Maybe I'm a clairvoyant.'

'Perhaps I am, too. I am even beginning to guess who you are. Soon I shall prove it.'

Kersten could not speak. His chest heaved up and down. How much did Heydrich know? More than he had to. None in the Reich were more resourceful or could create lies so methodically as he. He did not need the truth to capture Kersten. His cunning could alone do that. Kersten sat stunned, unable to move. Heydrich cared not so much about truth, but about his intentions that he put before anything. He studied Kersten without blinking. There was no point, Kersten thought, trying to find humanity in the man before him. If it had ever been there, it was now long gone. Not even a memory. This was why Kersten knew Heydrich was going to arrest him. Then the phone rang. Heydrich reached for it. He nodded and put the phone back on its cradle, looking at Kersten all the while.

'The Reichsführer wants you in his office immediately.'

Kersten rose. Chance, the final decider of events, surmounting both necessity and free will, had shown its hand. When Kersten reached the door he heard Heydrich's smooth voice.

'Don't worry; we will see each other again.'

CHAPTER 25

Schellenberg

Lieutenant Colonel Jerzy Soznowski admired his lavish ball room for what would be the last time. In five minutes he would have slithered out into the black car waiting for him that would take him back to his homeland, Poland. He would miss Berlin society, especially the women who loved him. He owed them for his success as a secret agent. Now, for a time at least, that was all about to end. His movie star face peered over the guests who sat in his drawing room, around a lavish stage in front of the window where a stripper rolled her hips to the band gathered in the corner in their tuxedos. Their faces were tight with concentration as they laboured over their instruments, playing Benny Goodman's Sing Sing Sing. Waiters in cream coats orbited tables where people cheered as the dancer, also a Polish agent, writhed under the lights. These workers in uniform made sure everyone's champagne glass was full while the night climaxed. The girl had just removed her bra, and was pulling the straps of her pink panties, arching her back as though she were thrusting the drumbeats, that clashed harder and harder. Her nipples were swollen like dark cherries in the glow of the chandeliers. The lights went dim. The crowd roared through tobacco smoke. The band played quicker and the dancer prowled across the floor on her hands. Actors, industrialists and politicians leant forward in expectation. They were consumed. They whistled, clapped and hooted. Time for Jerzy to exit.

He moved up to his room where he swept aside his curtains to look below. The black Rolls Royce was waiting for him in the dark, quiet side street, just as planned. There were no stars, only moonlight. Blue and pale like a mortuary. Only the glow from a street lamp creeping through the lace curtain in his fingers. He left his darkened room and jogged down the steps. The drums and the cheers began to wane behind him. He took the last two steps with one leap. When he ran through the front door he found himself in the cool night. Jerzy walked over to the car that waited for him. The windows were tinted and no one could see through them. Jerzy did not even bother to glance at his mansion as he opened the back door and sank into the Rolls. He had only just done so when he felt a pistol in his ribs. A voice he didn't recognize spoke to him in German. 'Welcome to the Gestapo.'

Heydrich and Muller leaned back in their chairs and toasted Walter

Schellenberg with their pints of Hoegarrden beer. They had chosen to dine at the Alexanderplatz because it was chic and appealed to their youth.

'I congratulate you Schellenberg for not only your kidnapping mission but for a fine story. You're as smart as everyone says,' Gestapo Muller said with a little clap. *Something isn't right*, Schellenberg thought. He felt like the men before him in their black, death uniforms were up to something. Muller sniggered silently. Schellenberg knew his story wasn't that amusing.

While Heydrich drank his beer he leered at the young, pretty waitress with straight blonde hair and a doll face who seldom smiled. She lowered her eyes and paced to the end of the bar. Only last week Heydrich had taken her out in the back alley, parted her thighs, and fucked her hard against the brick wall while he had smashed her face against it until blood ran into her eyes. She still bore the rumour of a black eye that embarrassed her.

'I'm honoured to serve my country, Herr Muller.'

'As am I,' Heydrich replied slowly, putting his glass down. 'Oh and by the way, are you fucking Lina.'

Schellenberg's thin, sensitive face went pale.

'Your wife?'

'Do you know any other Lina?'

'No.'

'Well that probably means we're talking about my wife. Don't pretend you don't know what I mean.'

'I'm afraid you're confused, Reinhard. I would never do such a thing.'

'Don't make me reach for my handgun,' Heydrich replied. Yet Schellenberg quickly retained his usual confidence. He shook his head with disbelief. His face was moist with perspiration. The atmosphere felt hot and intense like air over a fire.

'You have just drunk poison.' Heydrich hissed.

Silence. Finally Schellenberg laughed. Then Muller. Soon they were all laughing.

'I'm not kidding.' Heydrich said. 'It will kill you within six hours. If you tell me the whole truth, I'll give you the antidote.'

Muller leaned back in his chair. 'I had you followed. You took her to Pioneer Lake. Then what...'

Heydrich swirled the ice in the bottom of his glass. Finally, Schellenberg began speaking over the pulses of his heart, his eyes shining above his high cheekbones.

'We took some photos and then...we took a little walk and sat down beside the water for...no more than twenty minutes, talking about Wagner. I swear it was all very innocent. Then-'

'After the coffee, you went for a walk with the boss's wife.' Muller interrupted, his icy blue eyes shining like strange stones. 'Why are you hiding this? You do understand that you were being watched, don't you?'

'A fifteen minute walk was all it was, I swear.' Schellenberg replied, and then recounted what had transpired that day.

Heydrich leaned back in his chair, watching Schellenberg silently for a long time. Like a judge about to pass sentence. 'All right, I suppose I must believe you. But give me your word of honour that you will never do anything like this again.'

'Very well,' Schellenberg replied. 'But only after I drink the antipode. Otherwise, the oath would be worthless.'

Reinhard smiled at Schellenberg's boldness and poured a martini. 'Well I cannot totally blame you for your interest in my wife. But beautiful women do not last.' Heydrich said, sinking his hand into the pocket of his SS jacket. He removed a capsule that he placed on the table between them along with the martini. He let it sit there for a moment, as though to tease Schellenberg. Then he broke the tablet open and poured it into the drink. He rose and clapped Schellenberg's shoulder. 'Drink that and you'll be just fine.'

The drink tasted more bitter than normal. Schellenberg knew Heydrich was methodical as he was mad. The 'hangman' did not lie about such things. As he walked off he patted Schellenberg's shoulder and spoke without even glancing at him.

'Make sure you don't spill any.'

Schellenberg had had enough. The conversation with Ribbentrop still rang in his ears.

'Schellenberg, we have a genius plan.'

By us Ribbentrop meant the Führer and himself.

'Yes.'

'We want you to kidnap the Duke and Dutches of Windsor'

'You're not serious.'

'On the contrary.'

'What will the Führer say?'

'He thinks Operation Willi is a fantastic idea.'

Oh God.

At first Schellenberg thought he was dreaming. He had travelled to Ribbentrop's office where the 'old man' received him like he usually did: from behind his desk with his arms crossed. If Ribbentrop was an animal he'd be a greyhound or an ant eater. Maybe even a praying mantis.

The Nazi Foreign minister had a thankless job by any ones estimation, but the former champagne salesman did himself no favours by being a upstart.

'The British Secret Service is holding the Duke under surveillance. He is faithful to Germany and the finest Englishman I've ever met.'

'Herr Ribbentrop, may I-'

'Be quick about it.'

'In what way does the duke sympathise with us? And just how reliable are your information sources?'

'There is nothing else to say on that matter and nothing else you have to know.'

Ribbentrop breathed through his nose. 'Reliable circles of Spanish Society. Don't ask me anything more about that.'

'If the British Secret Service tries to frustrate the Duke in some arrangement, then the Führer orders that you are to circumvent the British plans, even at the risk of your life, and, if need be, by the use of force.'

'Do I understand that if the Duke of Windsor should resist, I am to bring him into this 'other country' that you speak of by force? Isn't that a contradiction?'

'The Führer feels that force should be used primarily against the British Secret Service-against the Duke only in so far as his hesitation might be based on fear-psychosis.'

Now he had heard it all. But Schellenberg showed no signs of surprise. He was after all an agent, a specialist in deception.

'Have confidence and do your best.' Ribbentrop said smiling. 'I will report to the Führer that you have accepted the assignment.'

Hitler seemed terribly enthusiastic about mission Willi. The plan went ahead. On Thursday morning on the 25 July, Schellenberg and his two escorts, Heineke and Bocker flew to Madrid.

While Schellenberg tried to convince the Duke to side with him, Germany prepared to invade Britain. The Luftwaffe would drop their bombs like meteors from the sky. Schellenberg composed a list of Englishman for the Gestapo to headhunt. This included names such as Virginia Wolff, H.G Wells, Aldous Huxley and Freud, who wouldn't escape them although he was already dead. Meanwhile, Schellenberg failed to manipulate the duke and to kidnap him. Instead the Duke sailed to the Bahamas to become governor general of the British Island colony. With ailing health and despair, Schellenberg transferred from counter espionage to foreign intelligence department. Things improved immediately. In June 42 British trained Czech underground assassins blew up Reinhard Heydrich's car. He later died in hospital from infections to his wounds. A precession including armed Waffen-SS guards holding aloft torches made their way to the castle of Hradcang where Heydrich's coffin, wrapped in an SS cloth reached its temporary home in the silent night. From there it travelled by rail to Berlin where Hitler gave a brief eulogy over it.

Schellenberg had one less in-house rival. He also gained closer access to Himmler who he wanted to convince into making peace with the allies.

Schellenberg couldn't let such fortunes pass him by. He had visions for Germany and himself. Only one problem remained: his stomach cramps. There was, however, maybe even an answer to this: Felix Kersten, Himmler's therapist.

The Hegenwald Zhitomir, Himmler's Ukraine headquarters and stone retreat, buzzed with energy. Schellenberg found it pleasant, almost peaceful except for the 1,000 soldiers who hovered over the compound that consisted of bunkers, barracks, a military cemetery, banquet rooms, an airport and Himmler's villa. The trees were leafy and towered towards the angry clouds that had followed Schellenberg for hours in the plane. There was a nearby village with small stone houses and dusty roads. If he had enough time he would perhaps visit it. It was refreshing at least to leave Berlin.

A young Gestapo officer greeted Schellenberg. He snapped his heels and raised his hand in the Nazi salute which Schellenberg reciprocated. They strolled silently to Himmler's lair. Schellenberg heard the loud banging of hammers in the distance. Clear and sharp as the sound of some bird. Construction was underway. He heard jeeps humming nearby like overgrown insects. A few drops of rain splashed on Schellenberg's black collar before he reached the steps that had been cut from rocks ascending to Himmler's cabin. Rain pattered against the leaves, rolling slowly from the officer's hat brim as he pushed open the door and nodded Schellenberg through.

There was a dark oak chair below the window and Schellenberg crossed the Persian rug to sit on it, resting each his hands on his knees, propping his elbows up. He saw his pale face reflected in the window looking back at him. Beyond that he saw clouds hanging so low they hid the tops of the pines. He heard the doorknob turn and the ring of boots. Himmler looked flustered. He waved Schellenberg over to sit with him at the long, ponderous table. Behind Himmler on the wall a Persian carpet was mounted. A plain white lamp sat at the end of the table that Himmler read by at night. Schellenberg noticed huge skull rings on the Reichsführer's fingers, and the skull broach. He was not happy. He thrust the report into Schellenberg's hand, as though he regretted having seen it. Then his face changed for the better. 'I hear you suffer stomach cramps. Is this true?'

Schellenberg nodded. 'Yes.'

'Then you must see Kersten. He's harmless. Although he does have one annoying habit.'

'Oh…'

'Every time he treats me he massages a life out of me.'

When Schellenberg emerged from Himmler's office he used Brandt's phone to contact the Kersten for an appointment. Agent Muller came in holding papers. He stood behind Schellenberg, grinning. When Schellenberg had finished he hung the phone back in its cradle. Muller's eyes followed him. 'So you're seeing the good doctor now. I have an entire dossier on him. I'll show the world what a spy he is.'

Schellenberg stood toe to toe with Muller. 'I hear Kersten is very smart. Tell me, what happens if you don't find what you're looking for.' Muller twitched his nose. 'I'll write a bestselling novel about him.'

Kersten arrived for his appointment. He asked Schellenberg to remove his shirt and lay down on the couch. Soon Schellenberg felt comfortable enough to talk with Kersten in earnest.

'You have many enemies here. Are you afraid?'

'Yes. But I must ignore them.'

'I know you've freed people from death camps.'

'You're not the only one. Now you understand why some would like to see me liquidated.'

'I want you to help me...'

'Yes...'

'I believe together we can convince Himmler to replace Hitler and make peace with the allies. I know you wield influence and can help me persuade Himmler to take this course.'

'It won't be easy. Hitler is his God.'

'But I have American connections. Himmler is naïve enough to believe people will forget his war crimes.'

'True...'

'I have a second plan, but it isn't going well.'

'Oh...'

'Take that report out of my shirt over there, Kersten. It's about the Eastern Front. I wrote it to paint as pessimistic picture as I could so Himmler would consider peace negotiations with the Allies.'

'Very brave of you, Herr Schellenberg.'

'Sun-tzu was right. War is deception. I risked being blindfolded to a stake and shot to pieces for 'defeatism' over that fucking document.'

'You wouldn't have been the first.' Kersten sighed, pulling a note from the pocket of Schellenberg's shirt. 'Is this the one?'

'Yes. Read what Himmler wrote on top.'

Kersten read it aloud. 'I wish to throw the person responsible for this report, as well as its contributors into concentration camps.'

Kersten laughed. 'You do need my help. I know just the man who can influence Himmler.'

'And who would that be?'

'An astrologer of course. Who else?'

~

Kersten arrived at Hatzwalde to find Wilhelm Wulff waiting on the bottom step. He was fair headed with blue eyes and a perceptive and honest face.

'Come in,' Kersten said. 'Elizabeth has cooked scones.'

The astrologer sat across from the large, sensuous vain man who was shovelling scones into his mouth. He liked Kersten and respected his shrewd, if limited intelligence.

'So you composed the charts I asked for?' Kersten asked, reaching for his coffee mug which had the Swedish coat of arms on it.

'Yes. There is danger ahead for Schellenberg. He's a sick man, isn't he?'

'Yes.' Kersten said, leaning forward with rising interest, putting his coffee down on the small table beside his armchair. 'And what about the Führer? Have you seen anything that may convince Himmler into replacing him?'

'Well, yes. Hitler will die just before May the 7h, 1945.'

'Brilliant.' Kersten said, smacking his hands together. Wulff, who somehow struck Kersten as a realist wasn't smiling. 'What is it?'

'Hitler has the same positions in Saturn in his natal charts as another military leviathan.'

'Who?' Kersten asked turning serious.

'Napoleon.'

'That we must keep between us.'

Schellenberg rang Kersten a few days later from Zhitomir where the plan to put Himmler into power to assist peace negotiations had claimed its name. The intelligence officer sounded impatient and wanted to know if he'd had luck with Wulff.

'I was just about to ring you. Good news. At first Wulff wanted nothing to do with it. He told me he didn't want the Gestapo to throw him back in prison. But then I convinced him he would be alright. I also talked Himmler into seeing him. They meet in two days here at Bergwald.'

'Splendid.'

So began Wulff's journey into darkness. He travelled in an unnecessarily expensive car via serpentine roads that wound up among hills and took him to Bergwald, Himmler's late Baroque castle which lay at the foot of Gaisberg. Wulff was impatient and needed to urinate badly.

At first the fortress revealed only the top of her spire through the trees. He passed a winding bend. And there it was: Bergwald, robed in sunlight, rising above the treetops. A beautiful wrought iron gate opened and the shining black Mercedes limousine glided through. Wulff peered through his window at the Salzburg Alps broken in the sky.

He arrived late to luncheon where Himmler rose to greet him warmly with a pat on the back. Himmler was a medium sized man with horn rimmed glasses who instantly struck Wulff as impressively mediocre. He had an orderly appearance that suited him. Wulff saw mundane cruelty in this dull, weary face. A mechanical heart full of magical spells put there by some genius.

Wulff sat at the oval, mountain ash table with Himmler and his guests who all looked at him shyly as though he were Santa Klaus. Two brutes with block heads and cat like jaws sat either side of him. Despite their beastly appearances, they still managed to eat with more manners than the Reichsführer.

Himmler resumed his discourse on spiritualism. His men listened in admiration. None more so than the secretary, Brandt, another mediocre man. He had sad, serious eyes that must have seen some terrible things. Wulff imagined he had no life apart from serving Himmler. Brandt sucked his soup like a peasant with his arms akimbo. He was not a man you remembered easily. Or wanted to.

After the tortuous meal, Himmler called Wulff into his office and shut the door. The Reichsführer leant on his desk and shook his head. It seemed he had planned something to say. 'The British are using pendulum diviners to sink our submarines. We need psychics to match theirs.'

Wulff didn't answer, as he settled in his chair. Himmler sat down and crossed his arms. 'We do our best, nevertheless. We want Germany to have a government for the people.'

Wulff tried to conceal his ironic frown. He did not like Himmler. *Just look at him*, Wulff thought. *A robot with horned rimmed glasses and a metal heart.*

'I'm sorry the Gestapo jailed you.' Himmler said. 'Astrology is too mischievous for common people.'

A pause. Himmler burped and excused himself. 'Kersten tells me you drew up the Führer's horoscope. '

Wulff only had a second to think. He stared at his knees. Then he lifted his eyes.

'It's true. And I don't like what I see. We are heading for great danger, Herr Reichsführer. Hitler will die just before May the 7th, 1945.'

Wulff had done what Kersten and Schellenberg had told him to. They instructed him to convince Himmler to overthrow the Führer by providing a horoscope that would bring only death and destruction to Germany. Himmler breathed through his nose. He rose to his feet and circled his table. *Like a shark*, Wulff thought. Then he paused and studied Wulff while he fiddled with his SS death's head ring. 'You know Herr Wulff, what we two are discussing is high treason. Hitler would have out heads for it.'

'Foreign opinion of you would change if you brought peace and shut down your concentration camps. Do not wait until it is too late.'

Himmler lowered his face pessimistically as though he were sinking into the fog of some dark thought which he could find no way back from. His arms stayed folded. 'If I do as you suggest, Hitler would hang me.'

Schellenberg lay out before Kersten who began rubbing the young man's back forcibly, driving out what Himmler called, bad spirits. Kersten was every bit as good as Himmler proclaimed. Kersten's fingers seemed those of a god, driving away the bad blood and replacing it with the good.

'It seems our work is doomed sometimes, doesn't it.' Kersten sighed.

'Yes. But we mustn't give up hope.'

'No, we mustn't.'

At the end of the treatment, Kersten reached into his coat. He held up some envelopes.

'I want you to send these to Holland.'

'Who are they for?'

Kersten smiled. 'My girlfriends...'

CHAPTER 26

Kersten had good reason to joke. Heydrich, who almost had him arrested and possibly killed, was gone. Yet even that had gone badly. The world discovered the venom of Nazi reprisal. On account of a false lead, an innocent love letter between a factory girl and her lover, the people of Lidice were held responsible, although not one of them was Heydrich's assassin. Almost every villager in the Czechoslovakian town was round up and shot. Not even the dogs escaped. The town was laid with salt so nothing would ever grow from the ashes of fires the SS ignited.

But retribution did not stop there.

Seventy four young women were mutilated in operations with injuries that replicated those that led to Heydrich's death. The doctors' aim was to prove the use of sulphonamides could not save these women who were injected with viruses that killed many of them.

Like a beast that grows a new head when its old one is severed, a new beast emerged to replace Heydrich whom some jokingly called Himmler's brain. This man already knew and hated Kersten with a murderous passion. One day, very soon, he intended to put this passion into use.

CHAPTER 27

Rudolf Franz Ferdinand Hoss laid his map before Himmler who leaned over and studied it. Bracht stood beside him, along with Schmauser and Kammler. The men nodded, their lips pursed as they heard Hoss brief them of problems at the camp that needed addressing: disease, needless death, and poor sanitation. Outside the death trains would be trailing their clouds of smoke across the fields and past the mountains. As the war raged on they seemed to come in greater numbers rumbling over the tracks until they reached the gates where the prisoners stepped into the raw light shielding their pale faces before gazing up at the sign on the gates inscribed with a simple message: 'Work makes one free.' Sometimes a sigh would go up among them.

The soldiers herded the prisoners into different directions to their fates. Those fit enough to work were sent to do so, the others sent to perish in the showers. Families clung to each other weeping and the guards ripped them apart, dragging them into the gas chambers. Showers would turn on and the people would scream. The naked Jews climbed on top of each other, making a mountain of squirming flesh. Through a viewing slit Himmler watched Zyklon B taking hold of the screaming lambs inside.

His face showed no expression and he said nothing.

Himmler had played a hand in this method of extermination. When near Minsk he had stood close to a pit trembling as the shot victims fell bleeding into the pits. At one point, looking green, he turned to Karl Wolff. 'A piece of brain just splattered in my face.'

Himmler crouched over and vomited. He decided to find an alternative method of execution. He quickly put his first idea to the test. His SS drove mental patients out amidst the pines. The guards herded the weak into a bunker packed with explosives. When the dynamite was detonated some people remained moaning after the smoke settled like an evil fog. Officers who could be seeing to other things spent hours recovering body parts from trees and bushes. Nazi officer Christian Wirth, in all his sadistic wisdom, chose a more efficient means of murder: gassing. Himmler was delighted. The Fuhrer would be too.

The doors to the chambers opened. Hands of loved ones and families joined grimly in death. The corpses were splattered with excrement, vomit, urine and menstrual blood.

Dozens of dentists converged like vultures forcing open the mouths of the dead with hooks to look for gold. Those that found gold teeth plucked them loose with pliers and hammers that they wielded joyfully. Some crouched over corpses eagerly pulling open rectums and vaginas to find hidden treasures. And the thieves held aloft their tins of loot and jingled them above their heads grinning all the while, their teeth flashing through darkness. Finally, Jewish workers dragged the bodies away by the heels through the mud. Trundles travelled all day to and from the crematorium bearing the corpses of children lolling about.

Himmler and his men trudged over the grounds observing everything. The Reichsführer raised his hat in the greasy air to brush away the flies that migrated from the nearby marshes. They passed the crematorium where Jew workers hurriedly sent the bodies of their family members to the flames. The victims were nearly all malnourished and as many as five could be hauled into one retort. The only time the workers got a break was when the chimneys filled with too much body fat and broke down. If the workers paused even for a moment, the SS officers would club them. So they toiled ceaselessly, their brows beading with sweat. The sour smell of bones clung to the worker's clothes long into the evening after the last knot of smoke rose into the sky like a crying soul.

Himmler passed the double story cement buildings and the garden beds where commanders yelled at the prisoners to cease digging and to stand to attention. They swiped off their blue caps and looked down at their clogs. A pitiful attempt at respect and dignity.

Himmler asked often about Dr Mengele, the prisoner productivity, and the epidemics that were killing the children. Himmler listened and his face did not change while his men informed him. So far, they told him, Mengele had tried several chemicals that he had injected straight into the prisoner's eyes to change their colour. Although none had yet worked, he remained determined that fortune would prevail.

When dusk came Himmler was passing the entrance where the orchestra played, poor fanfare pathetic in their rags. The Reichsführer ignored them. They were mostly Jews and weren't allowed to play German music, which Himmler believed was the only type worth listening to.

That night Himmler joined his entourage at a dinner party that with usual elegance included ribs, brown bread and Bavarian pudding. Among the guests was Carl Clauberg, the mutant whose feet did not touch the floor. He was so small and ugly that even his associates hated him. He watched Himmler with his usual adoration for the Reichsführer had permitted him to inject formaldehyde preparations into Jewish women's uteruses without anaesthetics. The doctor smiled abnormally like a pale faced clown. He swung his legs joyfully as though he was an overgrown child dangling his feet in water. Himmler had changed into a striking white SS uniform. He had swapped his muddy leather boots for clean ones.

Today he had snapped at one officer for not taking responsibilities of his problems, but now the Reichsführer appeared happy and calm. He sat at the head of the table.

The wax candles burned softly, the crystal and silver gleamed. Dr Werner Best's wife laughed loudly when he whispered into her ear, and kissed the back of her neck. She wore a necklace of diamonds. Himmler showed more delicacy than usual while he ate. Footman wandered in and out with dinner plates before clearing the table and bringing out the dessert. The guests wiped their mouths and lauded the meal. When they had finished eating ice-cream they began to smoke, drink and talk feverishly. Himmler began discussing his favourite subject: the Aryan race. Everyone listened intently, including the young servants with ambiguous expressions who came to refill the guests' glasses.

'The Nordic races were above pettiness, and strived to make the world better. Such was their purity, their sense of adventure, and benevolent bravery. You need only examine their tall frames, their pure eyes, their long craniums that bear such graceful, encompassing minds.'

Everyone listened. Himmler was at his most charming. He bent closer to a brunette who sat opposite him. This girl was Dr Werner Best's wife.

'Can you please light me, dear?'

'Of course, 'the beautiful brunette lent forward with her husband's lighter that she held beneath Himmler's cigar. He took a few puffs. When he was done, he leaned back and waited for everyone's opinion on the conversation that he had so kindly begun. It was the brunette who spoke first, although she did so only after painful hesitation.

'But if your Aryan doctrine is true, would you, Herr Himmler, Dr Goebbels and even the Führer not lose the leadership?'

Himmler smiled at what he conceived as the girl's sweet innocence. He blew a ring of smoke and ran his tongue across his thin top lip. Deliberately.

'In a round skull, such as my own, a long brain can be planted.'

The guests continued drinking silently until Rascher's wife, who was tipsy and sociable, raised her eyes. 'Tell us something more about the Nordic stories you love?'

Himmler eyes glimmered. 'Why not.'

So began the Reichsführer's dialogue. Unlike his Führer, he did not talk with rousing passion and energy, but with calmness and confidence, that was captivating in its own way. It was something Himmler had learnt in the old days. At such moments, one could have mistaken him for a priest.

'We're all familiar with Snow White. She was living in the Alps when the wicked queen in Rome plotted her downfall. The Queen would not cease her witchery until she was fairest and everything white was dead. One day, a peddler from a distant land gave Snow White a corset. But this was no peddler. The queen pulled the corset laces so sight, Snow White fainted and fell. Rome's emissaries had bound the Nordic spirit, suffocating it with alien concepts and deceitful words.

The dwarves, good spirits of the Folk, freed Snow White from the Sinai which fouled our Nordic blood. Next, the wicked queen used a magnificent, glittering comb to try and break Snow White's Nordic spirit, but this also failed for Snow White remained the fairest of all.

The Queen inspired by the infinite depths of envy, returned with an apple, and a very shiny one at that. The first bite stuck in Snow White's throat and caused her to faint as though dead. What does that apple mean? It represents the abandonment of our tribal ways, the rejection of our nature. Yet the story uses the term 'as though dead'. Thus the author acknowledges the time when the Nordic tribe will rise from its half-death, its sleep.

Until them, however Rome continues to wield her whip, alienating us from our ancestors.'

Himmler stared before him, as though he were searching for the past he longed for so badly. When he returned to the present, his tone grew stern.

'Rome's army is great, but freedom begins from within, not without. Stronger than any army is the man who wields the power which resides in him!

Often I've thought of the French monks, wrapped in their robes, trekking from Switzerland to convert our Nordic forefathers, the Goths and Vandals. Little wonder our ancestors thrust their swords in wraith at these idle, pedantic men. And yet over time the spirit of these forefathers became but dreams, whispering to our ignorant ears from the blood that our homeless hearts pump forth. We came to worship a God who despised his own creation and made them weak, small and humble before him.

To find the old blood that chased prosperity across the seas, one has to look for it in blue eyes that do not lie, but blaze with truth and the vigour of our ancestors. Such eyes as Erik possessed that laughed at death that would never have dared to look up into the clouds for a God to beg for mercy or help. When he seized his poisoned chalice he drank it with a smile, and probably rapped it with a fingernail, so that all could hear it was empty.'

Himmler paused to rap his glass that rang out loudly in the silence. The women smiled.

'He did not compromise himself for God. Erik knew everything necessary is good...'

'Sounds like Nietzsche's eternal recurrence,' the misshapen Clauberg said, leaning forward with his good ear that missed not one word his master spoke.

'What's that?' the lovely brunette asked, looking about the table for answers that did not come straight away for no one wanted to disturb

Himmler's speech.

'The idea that one lives life over and over again and that one should be prepared to do so willingly and gloriously despite all the pain and suffering that comes with it.' Dr Werner Best said. No sooner had he done so, then he returned his eyes to Himmler who had not finished.

'Like reincarnation?' the drunken girl blurted.

'Hmm, sort of,' her husband explained with a pained smile. Finally, Himmler continued, but only after he was sure no one else wanted to speak.

'One custom which remains with us in the North is naming. Our ancestors gave a child a name full of joy and energy. Actually, it was lent to them in the hope the child would live up to it. So the child bore it like a star he followed in the night. It was their sacred responsibility. This name strengthened the child. They became the name and the name became them.'

'That sounds like self-fulfilling prophecy?' the camp leader, Rudolf Höss asked. His comment surprised everyone, for although people thought him intelligent, they did not think him artistic or educated. What he lacked in imagination, however, he made up for in competency.

Himmler smiled.

'Exactly. And what names these people bore: Meinrad, Asmus, Bjoern. Peculiar names, certainly, but ones that taste of the sea and fruitful air full of sunshine. In other words, names of our homeland.'

Himmler stopped and looked about him. He waited until a waiter refilled the brunette's glass of vintage 1921 Zeltinger. 'But one seldom sees respect for these names nowadays.' The Reichsführer paused to let a tragic sigh pass his lips. 'They've fallen away in hearts taking with them our rightful destiny.' The Reichsführer nodded regretfully. 'Luckily, we had heathens fighting our Christian enemies with their own weapon. It was he who remained true, with neither the hateful sneer of the Sinai or the weak knees of Nazareth.'

Himmler paused. One half of his face was dark, while the other side was reddish from the candle flame burning on the table.

'No heathen has ever sought God. One does not seek that which dwells in one's soul. He never doubted. Doubt belongs to an alien God, an unnatural God, in other words, the Christian divinity which demands that highest of things, 'belief'. But belief should come automatically.

The Christian is an eternal doubter.'

Himmler sent his glare over the enraptured faces around the table.

'Can we trust someone who is disloyal to himself? Can a man who wishes to return to the dust be great? Can a man who loves a vengeful God who baptises us in sin before we even draw breath, can that man love the world? Yet Christians continue to crawl on their knees to this God. We heathens would never insult ourselves like that. We stand by our deeds with courage and do not repent.

Tell me, does it not seem strange that Christians were once the outcasts? When the time comes, let them bury their God in the sky where he belongs. He is not part of this world. And will we heathens forgive our Christian brothers? Well, only petty men pity those beneath them. Great men scorn them.

It's my task to remind future generations that blood is everything. We must preserve it so others, thousands, millions of years from now will honour and thank us. The only real man is one that acknowledges this, for he transcends time and only by doing that does he control his present.'

So ended Himmler's speech.

CHAPTER 28

Autumn came and Kersten once again found himself bent over Himmler's tiny frame that he moulded until it found a brief peace.

'Could you treat a man suffering from headaches, dizziness and insomnia?' Himmler asked.

'Yes. Who?'

'I will give you their name but you mustn't repeat it.'

Himmler threw his feet across the couch and buttoned up his shirt. He took a file marked 'geheim' or 'top secret' from his desk. He passed it to Kersten.

'In your hand is the report on the Führer's health.'

Kersten opened the file and read it. He found what he had been waiting for. It felt like the Gods had smiled upon him. He remembered his and Schellenberg's Zhitomir plot to convince Himmler to seize command.

'A man with syphilis cannot run a nation.' Kersten said, waiting for Himmler to roar in protest. But this did not happen. 'You could use your SS to overthrow him. Your men would follow you to hell if you so wanted.'

'How can I overthrow the greatest genius the world's ever seen?'

Kersten did not argue. Instead he left Himmler to his ringing phone while he checked for letters. Today, there was only one. But it was very important. When he opened it at home on his way to the front door he could not believe what he read. His mouth went awry and his eyes started to water. Tomorrow, he would confront Himmler about the reports before him.

Kersten watched his feet climb the stairs to Himmler's office. He found Himmler busy at his desk as usual. Many agents passed him in the wide corridors and on the staircase but he ignored them. His cane scraped on the marble steps as he walked. Anyone would know it was he who was coming just by hearing it.

Himmler greeted Kersten and undressed to his pants. Once Kersten began the treatment, Kersten spoke about what had kept him awake at night, staring into darkness that seemed to have no end.

'Is it true your ordering citizens in occupied countries to buy up all the food then ship it here?'

'Yes, to complement our supplies and to starve them. The farmers will survive but the workers, intellectuals and city people will starve. We will give the French gold if we have to. The perceived murderers will be pure-blooded French working the black market. Ingenious, isn't it. Our hands are clean.'

Kersten could not let this rest. Although he kept requesting, Himmler kept denying. One day mid- way through the treatment, Kersten's eyes darted towards the photo of Himmler's daughter that the Reichsführer kept on his desk. Bull's eye. Himmler loved children, and he had never turned away an orphan no matter busy he was.

'Think of the French mother and her baby contorted with cramps like you suffer. Except she has no doctor to help her or her child.'

'Yes Kersten, you are right. I shall outlaw all black market trading.'

Himmler smiled ironically. 'You're starting to influence me, you know.'

CHAPTER 29

Kersten flew towards Munich, his pace no faster than that allowed by Himmler's very slow plane. What it lacked in speed it made up for in reliability that suited Himmler and Kersten perfectly. He tried to be lulled by the flight but the loud, cantankerous drone of the jet engines would not allow it. Shining spots appeared in the blue sky in the close distance.

I wonder who they are, Kersten thought, leaning towards the window. Next he found himself thrown forward as the plane dove vertically. The aircraft shook violently as though it were having a spasm. When it ceased the pilot tottered out, pale and stunned.

'See,' he said pointing the fuse large where he ran his fingers until he stopped at two holes made by British bullets. They appeared where Kersten had leaned his head against the porthole.

'As trained,' the pilot explained, 'the gunner shot two bullets with one second pause between firing. That second had saved your life.'

The aviator took a flask of cognac from his coveralls. When he was finished Kersten seized it, threw back his head and poured so much down his throat he coughed for almost half a minute.

Berchtesgarden.

'You're escape was lucky.' Himmler said from his desk. Kersten was in Munich where he had been summoned. Despite the attack on it, the plane had landed on time. Kersten was still exhilarated about his close escape. The rumour of adrenaline still ran through his blood making him feel lucid and light. 'But here you escaped an even greater one. The Führer questioned me about you. People have accused you of being a double agent. I do not know who.'

A tongue is as dangerous weapon as any, Kersten thought grimly. Himmler heaved a gentle sigh. 'You are safe. For now...'

September 1943.

As advised by the Finnish ambassador, Kersten planned to make a general report to Helsinki. He was looking forward the trip, but he grew even fonder of the idea, when he was contacted by the Swedish ambassador, Arvid Richert.

'Swedish ministers would like you to stop at Stockholm on your way.

They want to interview you, privately and informally.'

'I do not know if I can do that.'

'Oh…'

'I will think of a way. Goodbye Richert.'

Kersten put down the phone in its cradle and sat staring at it. In only a second, a light bulb puffed in his head. He had a plan.

'The embassy tells me I'm to be drafted to Finland and cannot be returned.'

Himmler froze as he threw his shirt over his shoulder.

'There is a way. You could defer me for two months to treat the six wounded Fins in Sweden. They lack personnel and medical supplies to help them.'

Himmler nodded for this was true.

'Do you remember when you said, Finland will not declare war on account of you?'

'I might have said that.'

'Well if I cannot use force I will use diplomacy. Two months is all I ask.'

'Very well. Go.' Himmler sighed, buttoning up his jacket.

'I want to bring my wife and my three year old son. The other two older boys can stay at Hartzwalde with my sister, Elizabeth Lube.'

'I will miss you, Kersten. You must return soon as possible.'

CHAPTER 30

Kersten's chauffeur drove him to Tempelhof airport. His family would join in him in two days. Grey clouds about. Kersten pressed his face against his window and watched the streets fleeting by. Many of these avenues no longer had running electricity. The people looked haggard and tired for they were cold and hungry. The SS, however, did not treat them with compassion. They seemed to blame them for the Allies bombing campaign which was weakening the city. Kersten was glad to leave that world behind. He boarded the plane that flew him to Stockholm where his old Baltic friend, Delwig met him with open arms at the airport.

'Let's go get some real pastries.' Kersten said holding his belly.

Over their meal in a café, Kersten asked Delwig where he could safely store the suitcase at his feet that contained the reports he had promised to make for the Finnish embassy.

'The bank has a safe. We will take it there first thing in the morning.'

The morning sun was shining meekly when Kersten arrived at the bank. A short well groomed teller with a rat face and slick black hair spoke to him from his station. Kersten rested his suitcase on the bench before them.

'I'll get you the manager, sir.'

The manager soon arrived. He was a tall, shiny man with grey hair that he wore whipped elegantly over his broad scalp. He studied Kersten with his blue eyes. The manager seemed familiar about Kersten's background.

'Seal it with lead and imprint it with your ring which carries the coat of arms that Charles gave to your ancestor, Andreas Kersten.'

Kersten happily handed over his burden of secret documents and journal entries to a staff member who carried it down into the cellar.

As always, Kersten took his time away to visit old friends. He went to Danderyd near Stockholm to visit the Graffman family. He saw soaring trees and village homes stretched along the coastline and into the mainland where owls hooted and deer antlers zigzagged between the elms.

Frau Graffman came from Holland and her parents were Kersten's patients. Holger was a charming and intelligent Swede. 'Germany cannot possibly defeat America,' he said with quiet happiness. 'American technology and aircraft production are on a scale that will overwhelm Germany.'

They were chatting in the dining room when the doorbell rang.

'That must be Abram Hewitt.' Frau said. 'He's an American.'

A man with a greying goatee and a determined, intelligent face entered the room. He smiled and shook the doctor's hand. 'Guten Tag. Wie sind sie?' he said in perfect German.

Kersten found Abram Stevens Hewitt to be an agreeable man. Abram had close connections with the American Government, especially Minister Stettinius. He had another friend, General William, a hero of the Great War. Kersten agreed to treat Abram who was suffering from migraines and stomach troubles.

Nine days later, Kersten treated Abram at his home in Stockholm. It was on a quiet street not far from the sun starred sea. Kersten relieved Abram's sore and stressful body. Afterwards, as often happened with patients, Abram became relaxed and talkative. 'This war must come to end, Kersten.'

'I totally agree. Perhaps America could make peace with Finland. After all, they hate National Socialism as much as the rest of the world hates it. It's only our despair over our winter war with Russia that made us German allies.'

Hewitt pondered for a moment as he finished buttoning up his shirt. A Willow-Warbler peered at them through the window, swivelling its head, watching them from down its beak as though it were listening. 'It's possible,' he said. 'America sympathises with Finland. But Finland has to make the first move.'

Kersten smiled. The bird thrust its beak towards the heavens where it projected its wings. There was hope after all.

Hewitt lifted his head and watched the Warbler disappear into the grey sky. He shook his head ponderously. 'Sometimes I feel consciousness belonged first to the Gods, and by some strange mistake man became conscious to. Man wanted to be as God, for he had the consciousness of one, but he remains in essence an animal.'

Sunday came. Kersten returned to Danderyd to visit Graffman. They sat in front of the fireplace. The flames roared quietly in the dying ashes. Graffman's dark eyes looked glazed in the light of the fire. 'I see dark days ahead for Europe,' he said sounding like an old doomsayer, hunched over and stone faced. 'In my opinion, the West underestimates the power of the East,' he said. 'But I do not. So we must make peace now.'

'Can we talk with Hewitt about it?'

'Of course. He'll be here in an hour.'

And so he came.

'Guten Abend,' Hewitt said to Kersten. It was six in the evening. The men wasted no time. They spoke with quiet passion about the war. 'No one will make peace with Hitler.' Hewitt said. 'The Reich has to go to, including all its minions like the SS. America and England will supervise democratic elections. Nazis must face court on war crime charges.'

'That may be possible,' Kersten said. 'I can talk to Himmler about it, for

I think he is ready to discuss matters.'

Kersten knew that Himmler did not understand America on a psychological level. But he knew Himmler respected its massive industry and military strength. Kersten wrote the message beside the window of his lounge room where the light was good. He was so excited that he had burst through the front door and had forgotten to remove his fedora.

We have worked on proposals for peace talks. I beg of you not to throw this letter into your wastepaper basket, Herr Reichsführer, but receive it with humanity which resides in the heart of Heinrich Himmler. In centuries yet to come the gratitude of the world will still be yours.

Lose no time, please. Every day wasted means that thousands of Germans, English and Americans must die, every day brings greater destruction.

I send you points which may serve as a basis for peace talks which follow:

1. *Evacuation of all German occupied territories and restoration of their sovereignty.*
2. *Abolition of the Nazi party: democratic elections under American and British supervision.*
3. *Abolition of Hitler's dictatorship.*
4. *Reduction of German army and air force to exclude possible aggression.*
5. *Complete control of the German armament industry by the British and English.*
6. *Removal of leading Nazis and their appearance before a court charged with war crimes.*

The fate of the world is in your hands.

Kersten sent the letter through the Finnish diplomatic bag.

CHAPTER 31

Hewitt meanwhile returned to America. He met General William at a bar not far from base. Wild Bill threw his arms around Hewitt and smiled with his friendly face. 'Let me buy you a beer, Hewie.'

The men sat in the corner of the dim pub where country music played. They heard pool cues smashing balls together on tables beneath smoky lights. The men drank and were happy.

'Who's this Kersten guy, anyway?' Bill asked.

'He's Himmler's therapist.'

'Himmler's therapist. Now there's a thankless job. God, he must be a real swell fella.'

'He's a victim of circumstances beyond his control.'

Old Bull wanted to believe Hewitt. But he had not yet made up his mind.

'He is neither a Nazi nor Himmler's friend. He's moving to Sweden. Not exactly Nazi behaviour...'

'Go on...'

'Kersten, along with Schellenberg, have been trying to rally Himmler to gather up his SS and overthrow Hitler. Himmler is ready to negotiate.'

'No wait,' Wild Bull, said holding up his index finger. 'Does Himmler have the power to do that?'

'Kersten tells me there are two million men in the SS and three hundred thousand men in the Gestapo.'

Wild Bull sipped his beer and thought. He kept looking at Hewitt over the rim of his jug even as he drank. He slammed down his glass and wriggled his chin. The intelligence chief sat with his arms stretched out on the table. Wild Bull believed his friend who sounded excited. Hewitt removed his written report and handed it to Wild Bull who studied it with a half-cocked eye.

'It's all in there, Bill. Just remember, I'm doing this because I love my country. Not because I'm its agent. We both know I'm not that.'

Wild Bill put the note in his trouser pocket. 'Well it may help us understand those crazy Nazis and how they think. That way we may be able to infiltrate 'em.'

'Exactly! Do I have your word it will reach its destination?'

Wild Bull smiled. 'I promise on my mamma's grave, this report will be sitting on Roosevelt's desk this time next week.'

Two days later, Wild Bull arrived at Roosevelt's office. He spent only five minutes with the president, during which time he handed him Hewitt's report. Roosevelt frowned at it. 'Interesting, William. Very interesting. But how do we believe a man who is Himmler's masseur.'

CHAPTER 32

On the third day of Kersten's visit, a man in a dashing blue suit knocked on the doctor's door. Kersten invited the underlining in and asked him for tea that he refused.

'The Ministry of Foreign Affairs wants to see you, but informally at his house.'

'Where is it?'

The underlining smiled. He glimpsed Irmgard in the lounge room on her knees pushing around toy cars with her and Kersten's son. She saw him and smiled back. The underlining lifted his eyes.

'Would you believe it's just around the corner?'

Minister Gunther's house was as sober and majestic as Kersten expected. The rooms were large and austere, containing only some oil paintings of Swedish nobles who scowled at Kersten as though they were trying to make him feel uncomfortable, even from the grave. Christian Ernst Gunther father had been a Swedish diplomat. It sometimes seemed like fate to Christian that he found himself in this position. He had broad shoulders and a distinguished face. He spoke intelligently.

'Thank you for commuting sentences of our people the Gestapo arrested.' Gunther said solemnly folding his hands together on his lap, watching Kersten who sat across from him in the guest room.

'Every day the West pressures us to join them. This conflicts with our neutral philosophy. But we can help them in other ways. Our idea is to save as many people in the concentration camps as possible. Will you help us?'

'Of course.'

This was not the last meeting they had. They met several times over the next few days. During one gathering, Gunther rose from his favourite chair to look through the window at the street below where anonymous civilians drifted by.

'I've had talks with the Red Cross. Count Bernadotte will represent them, and serve as an intermediary.'

This was good news. But Kersten had other problems. He still had two sons at Hartwalde that he missed dearly. Irmgard often spoke about how she missed Ulf and Arno.

'Even little Andreas misses them, don't you my little boy,' she told Kersten holding their child who cooed.

So it was with pleasure that Kersten returned home from his meeting with Gunther with the news they would be leaving. It was all very well to enjoy a free city, but other needs were pressing. Irmgard was missing her dear 8 horses, 25 cows, 12 sows, 20 fowl and giant boar, Raymond.

The Berlin they came back to had grown worse. The people were green with cold and hunger. All of them wretched. Their breath steamed softly. Time was defeating them. Allie bombers were dropping cargoes of fire and steel in the unlighted streets. Even SS headquarters had taken a beating. The Russian invasion was failing. And as before, the Gestapo seemed to take it out on the civilians who they seized and hounded in the streets. They could arrest you for liking swing music if they so liked. Nothing had really changed. Just like the old days when the brownshirts ran wild; the men who raised their medieval torches when they had slithered like a giant serpent through Berlin. Men, who in retrospect were not avenging and solemn saints, but disgraceful, beer swelling, potbellied hacks. They were an embarrassment. Even Himmler had said so during therapy. 'Albert Speer told Hitler to march them at night.'

~

When Kersten had heard that the torture in the concentration camps was real, he accused Himmler of making executioners, not soldiers. Himmler's main recruiting officer, old Gottlob Christian Berger shared this opinion. Along with him, Kersten had Brandt who remained faithful to him from the beginning. Now that Heydrich was dead, Brandt warned Kersten about a new enemy, not as intelligent, but just as brutal. 'Beware that melancholy brute, Kaltenbrunner. He will have you butchered.'

It was true, of course. Heydrich's predecessor Kaltenbrunner was savage. But he had nothing on Kersten who only had one fear. On his estate he continued killing and eating animals. This infringed food rationing laws. Kersten contemplated how he would solve this problem. One day he arrived at Berlin headquarters as usual. Except today he hauled a suitcase stuffed to the point of exploding. While he climbed the stairs to the Reichsführer's office eyes glanced at him but he paid them no attention.

Himmler sighed. 'Tell your American contact Hewitt to keep in touch. I agree to peace with the allies. But I will not cease the war against the Bolsheviks. As for war crimes? We've committed no such thing. I will never, ever agree to such a thing. Not as long as I draw breath, Herr Kersten.'

The Reichsführer was so livid he could barely unbutton his shirt. This didn't surprise Kersten. For Himmler, the bonds of race were the great reality.

Once the treatment took effect, however, Himmler grew quiet and peaceful. Kersten felt the man's soul drifting away under the magnetism of his fingers. When treatment ended, Himmler seemed a different man. Kersten knew Himmler grew hungry at such times. He opened his case and removed a slice of bacon that he put on the Reichsführer's saucer. Himmler carved the meat with his SS knife. While he crunched down on the meat Kersten studied him.

'Would the Reichsführer like another?'

'Yes-he-would.'

Kersten laid another pork slice on Himmler's plate.

'Where did you get so much ham from?' Himmler asked chewing with an open mouth. In some ways he remained the ill-bred country boy he had always been.

'I slaughtered a pig on my estate.'

Himmler went stiff. 'You could be hanged for clandestine slaughter.'

Kersten pointed at the piece of meat on the end of Himmler's fork. 'Like the person who benefits from it.'

Himmler wiped his mouth with his SS handkerchief. He paced up and down... 'Ribbentrop will forbid you extraterritorial status.'

Kersten left smiling. When he returned the next day to treat Himmler, the Reichsführer handed him a permit allowing him extraterritorial status.

CHAPTER 33

June 1944.

Himmler travelled to Holland bringing Kersten with him. The public grew familiar with Kersten who often shadowed Himmler. Kersten was happy to return to where he could see all his old friends. He stayed at the Gestapo hotel. From there he often went to visit old friends. One seized him in the street but Kersten didn't recognise him.

Kersten reached for his wallet but the tall, gaunt man simply smiled and hugged him. 'Look Kersten,' he said, yanking off his black toupee when they were around the corner in an alley. 'It's me, Bartel.' Kersten's eyes welled with tears. This was one of his dearest informants: a university lecturer- an intellectual and therefore the Reich's enemy. He smelt of sweat and he needed a shave and a shower. He looked as though he was living out of his trench coat that probably contained things Kersten didn't wish to ponder.

How Bartel had changed. The friend Kersten knew had been athletic and olive. Nothing like the pale, shrunken specimen before him. This, it seemed, is what life under the Nazis did to someone. It crushed the life out of them as though it were draining them from the inside out. Bartel was very eager to explain himself. 'I've had to disguise myself to avoid the Gestapo. Informants are everywhere. I can barely trust a soul. Friends you've known for years will betray you for a scrap of food.'

Kersten remembered Himmler's proud words.

To rule Holland I need only 3,000 police and some extra rations-then the police know everything.'

The men strolled down the cobblestone alley. Cold walls with little sunlight. A few pools of old water.

'I know, I look thin, don't I?' Bartel said with a grim smile. 'But quite the contrary, Kersten. Since I've been obliged to fast my mind has been sharp and vivid as that of someone fifteen years younger. It's true. My wits are keen and my vision is clear as the sky. I piece things together quicker than I've ever done.'

Bartel gave a little laugh. 'You probably think I'm mad, because I know how much you enjoy the good life; good food, good women, eh.'

Bartel, emboldened by lonely pride, slapped Kersten's shoulder like a cheeky schoolboy. He paused to look over his shoulder. 'You're doing a fine job, Kersten. But tell me, what is he like?'

'Who, Himmler?'

'Yes. Germany's grim reaper.'

'Well like I tell everybody else. He reminds me of a respectable clerk, a schoolteacher or maybe even a headmaster.'

Kersten performed his daily treatments at Seyss Inquart's house where Himmler was staying. Seyss appeared after one session with a bow. Like a messenger addressing their emperor he had come with information that excited him very much. He read out the names of people who were to be arrested tomorrow morning. He wanted Himmler to know what a fine job he was doing. One name he read out, resonated like a bell tolling in Kersten's head: his old friend, Thurkow.

Heydrich Himmler had no idea of Kersten's pain. He was looking himself over in his mirror, buttoning up the collar of his shirt with his nimble fingers.

'So you won't come to Mussert's party? His new house is very luxurious. You will love it, Herr Kersten.'

Kersten didn't even try to hide his grief. The house belonged to Kersten's old dear friend F.T who was simply kicked out. And now the poor fellow was about to be arrested. After that, the Germans would more than likely kill him.

'I wasn't invited'

Himmler tugged down his jacket and straightened his cap. 'You can go wherever I go.'

'Thank you, but I have other plans.'

'Suit yourself.' Himmler said and strolled outside where his chauffeur waited. Soon Kersten was in his chauffer. Yet the mood he experienced at his friend's new house would have been very different from the one Himmler would be enjoying. The mood was surreal. Both men knew what was coming. Still, they sat and chatted long into the night. They did not talk alone. Mr de Beaufort came with his beautiful wife. They were part of the Resistance. Beufort talked energetically about his organisation. The blood rose to his face and his eyes shone like flashing blades. His wife sat beside him smoking a cigarette from an ivory holder, one long leg cocked over the other. She watched everyone carefully from beneath her long lashes but said nothing. When the eleventh hour neared, Beufort revealed the urgency and desperation of his plight. He understood the dangers facing him. Possibly, even death. He handed Kersten a letter. The doctor gazed into the resistance fighter's sparkling green eyes.

'I want you to send this letter to Sweden where my people will mail it to London. Can you do that please?'

Beufort did not blink. He looked so tired. Exhausted.

Kersten held the letter to his beating chest.

'I will.'

The drive home was gloomy and silent. Kersten looked out at the darkness and he wondered if all this pain would end. And if it did, would he be alive to see it. This is what everyone thought, of course. No one felt truly safe. The threat of prosecution had become a shadow that followed people wherever they went. Everything looked suddenly mournful: the oak trees, the moon and the lights at the windows of houses where people lived in fear. Kersten was listening absently to the quiet roar of the Mercedes motor when he paused.

'Driver, please stop at headquarters.'

The driver pulled up with a slight screech before the first police guardhouse where a tall man bent down to speak to Kersten who lowered his window. The officer wore his hat pushed down to the bridge of his nose. He examined the special pass Kersten handed him. If Kersten was to save his friend it had to be tonight. Tomorrow, it would be too late. The guard held the paper out before him. He studied Himmler's signature down the bottom corner of the page. The guard lifted his eyes. 'You're in luck. He returned ten minutes ago.'

The guard touched his hat brim, nodded gravely and the car drove on.

The chauffeur pulled up on the gravel driveway that crinkled beneath them. He killed the lights. Kersten threw out his legs and leant forward on his cane as he emerged from the car. He travelled faster than his legs and staff would like. He mounted the stone steps to the main doors that he threw open like a man on some divine crusade. In the distance he heard howling dogs.

Himmler was leaning on his bed removing his shoes when Kersten entered, slightly out of breath leaning on his cane. The Reichsführer looked up, his eyes red and tired from socialising. But when he saw Kersten his face beamed and he smiled.

'You must be a mind reader. I was going to call you. But then I thought my cramps weren't bad enough to wake you.'

'I feel it, and here I am.'

Kersten removed his hat and put it beside him on the oak table. He also leant his cane against it that was still trembling in his hand. Soon he was once more working his magic upon Himmler who gritted his teeth with pain and closed his eyes as he felt familiar peace rush over him-a wave of it, and he closed his eyes as though he were diving into it.

'I don't even have to summon you when I'm in pain. You know it.'

'This morning, I heard Seyss Inquart telling you about twelve Dutchmen who were to be arrested tomorrow. One of them is my friend, Thurkow. In fact, most of them are my friends.'

Himmler went red and screamed. 'They are traitors.'

'Please, stop this. It's madness. I know these people. They are innocent.'

'That is what you always say.'

'Because it's true.'

Himmler straightened his glasses. 'Oh, alright. What does twelve men matter? I'll call tomorrow.'

'But by then it will be too late. It must be now, tonight.'

'Reuter will be asleep.'

'He'll wake up.'

Himmler frowned like a disappointed child forced to confess their indiscretion. 'You always have your way.'

Kersten waited not one second more. He dialled the number and waited. Perhaps Rauter had gone to bed. Maybe it was too late.

Rauter wasn't asleep. He was with Berger having a quiet drink when the phone rang out. When Rauter hung up he looked angry, disappointed and shocked. Berger knew something was wrong. Rauter stood frozen with his hand still holding the phone in its cradle.

'Kersten is dangerous. I'd like to know who's behind him.'

Berger shrugged. He was sat at the table over his beer.

'You're not smart enough, Rauter. Kersten has a longer reach than you. Himmler will only see you after a formal request, and in uniform. Kersten is in his room right now, seeing him in his nightshirt.'

Kersten had had a tiring night. It was past 1 am. He lowered his head into his hat, took his cane and opened the door leaving Himmler to sleep. He had gone only a few steps when he heard the door open behind him.

'I almost forgot.' Himmler said, dressed in his nightshirt. 'Seyss gave me some apples and chocolates. Please have some?'

Kersten didn't need to deliberate. He took as many apples that would fit into the pockets of his coat where he also manage to stuff two chocolate bars. Himmler crouched on the corner of his bed, wrapped in his flimsy night shirt. He lifted his arm slowly as if it were a heavy weight and rubbed his eyes. He pondered into space. 'I should have resettled the Dutch back in 41.'

'But you were so sick. The sickest you've ever been. You would never have been able to do it.'

'Yes, I owe my health to you. And you need not worry about your friends. No harm will come to them.'

CHAPTER 34

The following day Himmler and Kersten flew to Berlin. Both men sat calmly, each with both hands on their knees, each with an identical suitcase before them. One was full of Gestapo decisions, the other carried mail from the Dutch resistance.

The skies over Berlin were blue. The sun shone mildly. Kersten leant against the porthole clasping his saggy chin, thinking. He was strangely relieved to be home. He missed his family. And he was satisfied with the job he had done, the lives of the good people he had saved.

Kersten did not stay long in Berlin. He arrived to the airport with Irmgard close at his side. They held up their identification to Airport security. The officer glanced backwards and forward at the couple as he read their Identifications. Kersten understood and smiled salaciously.

'Come through, Mr. T. M Kivimakki and Mrs. Kersten.'

Kersten walked through the gates carrying his briefcase containing the letter from Beufort that he had promised to deliver. Irmgard was happy to visit the city she planned one day to make her home. Once more, Kersten made his way to Gunther who accepted him with a firm handshake at his door. He looked the doctor up and down. 'You look strong and healthy.'

'Fat you mean.' Kersten laughed.

The men wandered into the drawing room. The weak morning sunlight drifted through the window where Gunther had stood when they first met, reflecting which was his way.

Kersten got right down to business. 'I will get to work, but I need two things.'

'Go on.' Gunther said leaning back in his chair.

'Recognition of my doctor's degree in Sweden. And an apartment in Stockholm. My family and I wish to make our life here.'

Gunther nodded. He leant out of his chair and shook Kersten's hand. 'Agreed.'

'My plan is this,' Gunter said relaxing back into his chair. 'We must get the Norwegians and the Danes out of the concentration camps. They should be sent to Sweden who will intern them until the war ends. If that is not possible, Sweden will make camps where the Swedish police would guard them guaranteeing they would not return home before the end of the war.'

Kersten reflected. 'The Swedish rescue campaign is necessary. But many Nazis are against it: Goebbels, Ribbentrop and Kaltenbrunner. On the other hand, if given enough time I may be able to convince Himmler who shows signs he is weary with bloodshed.'

'Then it is up to you, Mr. Kersten, to use those miraculous hands of yours.'

Kersten nodded as though he saw no untruth in Gunther's description of him.

'One more thing…' the ambassador said moving to his desk where he took a note that he handed to Kersten. 'That's a list of eight imprisoned Swedes I wish you to save.'

'I shall do my best.' Kersten said with a distracted smile. He clipped open his suitcase which he had put on the coffee table. He removed from it the letter that had come all the way from Hague. 'Something a friend gave me to pass on.'

Gunther took the letter. Kersten clipped up his suitcase, swept it up and walked towards the doorway where he turned and tipped his fedora.

'Good day, Christian.'

When Kersten's car pulled up the driveway at Hartzewalde, a mob was waiting to greet them. Elizabeth stood with the children beneath her arms. The witnesses stood either side of them, smiling and waving as the Kersten's emerged from their Mercedes. The boys did not wait. They ran and hugged their parents. Kersten held his youngest high as he could before kissing his cheek.

Kersten knew better than to wallow in pleasantries. No joy can last forever. Perhaps, only misery can last that long. The following morning, Kersten rang Himmler. The Reichsführer sounded suspicious and aggressive.

'Katlebrunner scared me. He said you rented an apartment in Stockholm.'

'It's true.' Kersten replied. 'Cheaper than a hotel.'

'Yes, it is.' Himmler said with a laugh.

Himmler's headquarters in East Prussia were crude and depressing. It was constructed near the railway tracks in the forest. At night the goat willow branches drew a manic cobweb on his windowpane. Kersten had to accompany him to this doleful place. He waited for it to rain and it did. With the passing of rain came the passing of days, soaking the earth and soaking Kersten's soul. It poured thick as bullets slanting in the wind. While he massaged Himmler's pain and grief away, Kersten held up his long face. He looked as though he were gazing an abyss. Himmler was resting on his cheek with his eyes closed. But he could see the fat man's blue eyes turn cold. Something troubled him.

'The war will last longer than expected. What good are those Germanic people the Danes, Norwegians and Dutch dying in the concentration camps. You are one of Germany's greatest leaders and one of the world's most intelligent men. Make use of it and free your people.'

'But the Führer-'

'You would make a far better Führer.'

Himmler did something he had not done before. He seized Kersten's wrist. 'Do you really believe it?'

Kersten knew flattery extends far, but he wondered if he had overstepped the mark this time. Himmler, who was as careful a man as any in the Reich, saw Hitler as an unstoppable God. Himmler in all his fatal indecision still could not make up his mind.

'I tell my men, loyalty is everything. I tell them that every day. How then could I do what you ask?'

'Is serving a madman loyalty? You saw Hitler's medical file. Don't be foolish. You're time has come. You know it.'

Kersten pressed harder with his fingers and palms as though he were driving the point home.

'Listen to me. Give me Norwegian, Dutch and Danish prisoners.'

'But...'

'You're the only person in Germany who can converse in secret with the Swedes. They do not understand what you're doing to their blood brothers in the concentration camps. They will declare war on you.'

'We're still strong enough to handle them. But if you desire it personally...'

'I do...'

'Then give me time. These matters are never easy...'

CHAPTER 35

In Berlin, Kersten found a letter waiting for him in Himmler's post box. He pulled it out, slipped it into pocket of his coat and strolled down the steps leaning on his cane. Otto, his driver met him downstairs. They drove along the Oranienburg route to Hartzwalde where they pulled up at the front door. As soon as Kersten put his foot out he ripped open the envelope and stood reading the letter. A smile lit up his face.

Some people had written him a letter thanking him for saving their lives. It had been signed by eight Swedes: Carl Herslow, Tore Widen, Einar George, Stig Gronberg, Stig Lagerberg, Beglind and Haggberg.

Kersten sung to himself as he mounted the steps to his house where his boys waited eagerly to greet him.

June 1944.

'Yes, I must generous to the Germanic race.' Himmler said while Kersten massaged his pale flesh. Kersten knew he was making progress, tunnelling deep into Himmler's mind, his fingers weaving a spell as discreet as night.

'And the French, Reichsführer. You can save many of them from your camps. You said you are Henry the Fowler's reincarnation.'

'We'll see…'

Kersten celebrated with an extravagant meal in his carriage aboard Himmler's black train. He buried his roast chicken with gravy and tore it apart with his short, strong, powerful hands. He ate until he could eat no more. Kersten sighed and laid back in his seat. His mouth glistened with fat. It was time to sleep. And sleep he did. A profound sleep that contentment brings. He snored at the ceiling laid out on his back like a beached whale with his mouth wide open. Soon his eyes were shuddering. He saw his family on board a plane flying over the soaring Switzerland Alps whose tips were caked with snow. Kersten was breathing in the pure, lofty air when he heard his door tear open and he returned to his body with a jolt. Himmler's driver, Sturmbannführer Lukas hovered in the doorway, pale and breathing heavily.

'Get up. Someone has tried unsuccessfully to take the Führer's life.'

Kersten froze. 'Oh God…'

Just when things were going well, fate had intervened. How many lives would have to pay? Kersten threw his legs over the bed and thrust his feet into his shoes. He swiped up his overcoat and wrapped it around his shoulders as he strolled out the door.

A large sentry of SS guards was assembled outside Himmler's car, choking up the slim corridor. They were holding rifles and looked even sterner than usual. Their hooded eyes passed over Kersten who held up his pass beneath the nose of a tall young man surmounted by a black SS helmet. The guard had a face like granite, as though it had grown out of his hard hat. He nodded austerely. The doctor entered Himmler's office without knocking.

He found Himmler bent over his desk feeding documents through a shredder. He lifted his head only for a moment to glance at Kersten. He was so preoccupied with his thoughts and worries that at first he looked straight at Kersten's face without recognising him. 'Colonel Wehrmacht tried to kill the Führer. Now my hour has come. I've been ordered to arrest 2,000 officers.'

Kersten frowned regretfully. 'Whom do you propose to arrest? Are you sure of who they are? I hope you won't get hold of the wrong people, Herr Reichsführer.'

Himmler said nothing.

'Won't some of your intelligence workers be blamed?'

Himmler didn't seem to care. He was totally at the mercy of his determination and what lay before him. Kersten was stunned by the irony that Himmler earned his master's gratitude by providing him protection, and arresting suspected plotters. Now Himmler's empire had to punish itself with blood for the role it failed to fulfil. All to answer to the needs of Hitler to whom it ultimately owed its existence.

Kersten watched the papers disappearing into the teeth of the machine and with them his hard work. So many dreams dissipating as the wind dissipates smoke.

'I'm destroying your correspondence to Stockholm. One never knows...'

Kersten slumped in the air chair, deflated. He shook his head, smiled bitterly and gazed into the space. 'It's too bad they didn't get him. Our mission would have been easier.'

Himmler held himself to his tallest height. He looked injured and pale. He was eager for Kersten to hear his intentions. 'I'm more loyal to the Führer than ever and I will kill all his enemies. It is the will of Providence that Hitler has lived so we will win the war.'

'Then you will have to kill 90% of Germany.'

Himmler lowered his grey eyes and continued his work as though he hadn't even heard Kersten.

'Take the train and wait for my instructions at Hartzwalde.'

Himmler left his office holding the last of his papers. Kersten remained staring at the Reichsführer's desk which had been emptied of its secrets.

Hitler gave Himmler an arbitrary quota of flesh to fill. This meant innocent lambs would also lose their heads at the gallows. Death's gigantic sickle swept across Germany at frantic speed. Himmler carried through his task with all the righteous temper of his heart, and passion that came with being assigned such an important operation. The SS rounded up people in their beds. The Gestapo broke into their homes and dragged them away in front of their children. Some officers saw it coming, and they shut themselves in their officers or studies and swallowed their pistols and they released the triggers until their brains burst through the back of their heads onto the wall behind them. SS crazy with bloodlust and rage cut the genitals off their victims and shoved them in the mock grinning mouths of the corpses. Axes fell and bones snapped. Men were forced to offer their necks to the guillotines that plunged all day long splashing blood. Bodies hung from the front of butcher stores, their bare feet jostling in the cold wind, their eyes downturned. Himmler was a man with purpose and his thirst for running blood would destroy Kersten's plans.

CHAPTER 36

For many weeks Kersten heard no word from the Reichsführer. Himmler's new mission must have invigorated him, Kersten thought while he relaxed at Hartzwalde where an old patient visited him: Frau I. Direktor of St. Gallen. It was the third day in August. She looked thinner and more intense than when Kersten had last seen her. But this is what happened to everyone in war. She had withered legs and small feet. His friend had come not only for a social visit, but for something much more important, as Kersten was about to discover.

She sat with Kersten in the drawing room, removing her ribboned hat that she beside her on the arm of the chair. She looked very petite in that chair that seemed to have swallowed her.

'Some Swiss industrialists are joining with the International Red Cross in a scheme to get twenty thousand Jews from concentration camps and take them to Switzerland. They would be transported from there to the South of France where they would be held until the war ends.'

'And you want me to convince Himmler this is a good idea.'

Frau coughed into her hand. 'Yes, that is what I wish.'

'Then your wish is granted, Frau.' Kersten said bending down to kiss his friend's hand. Her eyes welled with gratitude and she burst out laughing, and he did too.

Kersten did not wait. He drove to see Himmler the following day. The Reichsführer, who was working busily in his office, raised his head from a paper in his hand while Kersten explained his plan.

'I already know about Frau I.'s activities. She has made attempts as this through both me and the Foreign Office. On both occasions, Hitler in all his wisdom and genius, intervened and stamped out her actions.'

'I know a Swedish Foreign Counsellor who will be very happy to talk with you, Herr Himmler.'

'Please…'

'These are lives at stake, women, children…'

'Enough. It's beyond my comprehension why you exert yourself so much on the Jews' behalf. Surely, you don't think that a single Jew will thank you. One day you will learn to know the Jews…'

Kersten was pondering this when an officer knocked at Himmler's door.

'Come in.' Himmler said. The tall, blonde boy entered. Himmler preferred to surround himself with Aryan types.

'Herr Himmler, a Mrs Huber is downstairs making a scene. Her husband was one of the men you liquidated over the Hitler assassination attempt.'

'Tell her that fate has dealt her a blow and she deserves to be upset-but she must remember the needs of the state transcend any human destiny.'

The officer raised his arm and stamped his right foot on the ground like a horse, gazing ahead with his blue eyes. 'Heil Hitler.'

The officer turned on his heel and was about to leave when Himmler called him back.

'In fact, I want to see this woman.' Himmler said rising from his chair. 'Can you wait for me, Kersten?'

'Certainly.'

Himmler shut the door behind him. Kersten stood up. He paced around the room. He noticed Himmler's bottom desk draw, the one he kept locked was open. Kersten peered closer. He saw a letter Himmler had written to his wife, Marga.

I'm off to Auschwitz, Kisses, Yours, Heini.

Kersten dug deeper. He saw a black folder masked 'Classified.' Kersten leant over Himmler's desk and opened the file. He had never done such a thing before.

Kersten studied the dossier. *Reports on the Führer.* Documents came no more secret than these. Himmler must have been reading them. Kersten found a copy of a letter sent to Boorman marked January '44. The memorandum contained a list of Hitler's cousins on his father's side. Paternal cousin Joseph Valet had a twenty one year old son who committed suicide, and three severely retarded sisters, one of whom Hitler had liquidated in an asylum. Hitler's two sisters were mentally deficient and caused him great embarrassment. At the back of the folder he found a report. It contained a name typed in large letters: Rene Mueller. She had been Hitler's lover. She had given someone intimate details of their affair that had ended up in this report. Hitler made her kick him mercilessly while he grovelled on the ground, naked. At the end of the page Kersten saw an undated endnote: Death by suicide. Another lover, Geli Raubal, Hitler's half-sister's daughter had also shot herself, although there was a question mark next to her name. *Foul play, perhaps,* Kersten thought?

Himmler had done his homework. His obsession with meddling into people's personal lives had paid off. Now Kersten knew why Himmler took the plot to replace Hitler seriously. Kersten had been more right than he first thought. Hitler was insane. Himmler wanted to help his Führer who was in bad health and he wanted to guide his country to victory. A mad man was running the nation. And he had been mad from the beginning.

The theatre of the absurd was real as the air Kersten breathed. Circumstance had given Himmler more justification to conspire against his

Führer than Kersten could have ever come up with. Where Kersten so far had failed, fortune may yet win his battle for him.

Kersten grew flustered. Footsteps were coming. He shut the folder and slipped it into the draw. The door opened and Himmler entered, noticing the uncomfortable silence.

'I just remembered.' Kersten said, touching his head. 'I have to treat Schellenberg in an hour.'

Kersten consulted his watch. Himmler raised his chin. 'Very well. I shall see you later, good doctor.'

CHAPTER 37

Kaltenbrunner

The spy had worked for Himmler for many years. He worked under Schellenberg but it was Ernst Kaltenbrunner who appealed most to his fanatical, Germanic heart. For that reason, he sided with the Austrian. Kaltenbrunner was uncompromising. When Hitler sent Hungarian admiral Horthy home in a locked and sealed boxcar he trusted none other than Ernst to overlook its return.

The agent sat across from his hero who was putting down on his desk the information that he had delivered in a sealed paper folder. The spy watched it sitting there on Kaltenbrunner's desk.

'You are positive that this is the route Kersten takes with his chauffer?' Kaltenbrunner asked stroking his chin formidably, hammering his index finger on the envelope.

'I've no doubt. He's been travelling through Oranienburg for years. It isn't much of a secret. This is actually one of my easiest missions, Herr Kaltenbrunner.'

'Yes, yes.'

Kaltenbrunner leaned back and gazed through his window where the sunlight rippled across the lace curtains. He made a pyramid with his hands and rested his chin upon them. 'There is no human law, or law of God or national law that states that any healthy being has to permit the snake to eat the mouse-but on the other hand, it is perfectly justified to defend the mouse.'

The spy watched Kaltenbrunner curiously. The chief leant his long, slender frame forward in the chair that creaked beneath him. He opened the folder again, removed a map that he laid out and studied. The spy watched his master's eyelashes blinking.

'Here,' Kaltenbrunner finally said pressing his finger down on the map at a specific spot, a forest bordering Ruppin. 'We strike here.'

The spy leant forward. 'You are familiar with it?'

'I am a chief for the secret police. Of course I'm familiar with it. It is perfect. There is a clearing. On both sides of the road there are lots of trees where we can hide our men. I'll post a German officer on the road to. He will flag down the car and ask for their papers. They will provide them of course, but we will not let Himmler know that. We will say they sped away from the checkpoint.'

'That is another problem. Himmler adores Kersten. What if he doesn't believe us?'

'We'll just plant a gun and say Kersten tried to shoot one of our men.'

'But so many bullet holes-'

'Look, I told you when we began this mission that I didn't give a fuck about Himmler. Remember?'

'Yes. Well, I think the location is perfect.'

'I didn't ask your opinion. I'm telling you, that is where we ambush that cunt Kersten. Now, I ask you one more favour.'

'Anything.'

'Give me a list of forty top SS men you know are on our side. I don't want Schellenberg to catch on. That would ruin everything. From this list I will select twenty men who I can trust. It is these men who will bury Kersten. Understood?'

'Yes sir.'

'Leave me alone.' Ernst said with a wave of his hand. The young spy rose and marched to the door. He turned his head when he heard Kaltenbrunner speak.

'The quicker humanity advances, the more important it is to be the one who deals the first blow.'

When things are bad, eat, Kersten told himself, ignoring that he indulged his appetites no matter how things were. The day was cheerful and sunny. He had slept well and he decided to eat out with his family. Irmgard had dressed Ulf, Arno and Andreas in pretty little boots, hunting caps and overalls. After their pasta, they ate ice cream from cones that pleased them greatly as it did their mountainous father. Things were tougher, even for them. To eat out was a treat nowadays.

There was no talk of war or Hitler. Instead they chatted about their farm animals, school and friends. They returned home refreshed and happy. Irmgard kissed Kersten's lips. 'We shall see you in two weeks, then.' What neither of them knew was the ambush waiting for Kersten that day. Twenty of the Gestapo's finest were waiting in the bushes as Kaltenbrunner had planned. They leant over their submachines in the bushes, resting the barrels against the trees while they crouched in the dirt, blinking like owls. Everything seemed more silent. Their eyes remained fixed on the intersection where in only minutes Kersten would arrive with his chauffeur.

Kersten strolled outside casually to where Otto waited to drive him to Himmler's train. He heaved open the back door to sink into the car when he heard an explosive roar approaching. An SS officer on a motorcycle, covered in dust and sweat, stopped right at Kersten's feet. He handed Kersten an envelope from his shirt. 'Very important letter from colonel Schellenberg, Herr Doctor.'

Kersten waited until the SS officer was almost out of sight to read the letter. Two letters were folded inside, but Kersten saw only one. The other one he let fall to the earth. What Kersten read made his heart race.

'Look out… Kaltenbrunner has decided to kill you in spite of Himmler.'

Kersten looked about but saw no one. He sank into his car and was about to close the door when he saw the second note lying in the dust. He picked it up.

'Don't take your usual route through Oranienburg. Take the other way, the one through Templin. You risk death if you go the other way.'

Kersten's head spun. He bit his bottom lip. Schellenberg was his friend, but he was ambitious. This made him untrustworthy. Perhaps the message was a double deception. Maybe the warning had come from Kaltenbrunner and his cronies. Moments passed while Kersten pondered. He closed the car door.

'Otto, we won't go through Oranienburg today. We'll go through Templin. For a change.'

The driver released the handbrake. Kersten brooded about his decision. 'On second thoughts, we'll take another route. Turn to the left and I'll show you from there.'

Otto glanced at Kersten in the rear view mirror.

'Is everything alright, Mr. Kersten?'

Kersten almost laughed. 'Apart from the day I was almost shot down by British pilots this could be my best day ever.'

CHAPTER 38

The Reichsführer swung his legs up over the couch and proceeded to dress with great speed. He did so because he was angry. Kersten had finally told him about the ambush.

'We're going to eat. Kaltenbrunner will join us.'

And so he did. He sat beside Himmler across from Kersten who nudged in beside Berger. They were in the restaurant cart that was Kersten's favourite.

'I hear you bought an apartment in Sweden. You must have a lot of wealthy patients there.' Kaltenbrunner said.

'No, I don't work there,' Kersten replied.

'What were you doing?' Kaltenbrunner asked.

'Don't tell me you didn't know. The British Service has been paying me to kill Reichsführer Himmler. I haven't succeeded, so I lost my job.'

Kaltenbrunner's jaw dropped. A waiter arrived with their meals almost froze when he overheard the therapist.

'Worse still, because of you he almost lost his job here.' Himmler said moving his spectacles up and down the bridge of his nose. 'You would not have survived Kersten by an hour.'

Himmler lifted his wineglass. Everyone else followed suite, except for Kersten who didn't drink. Kaltenbrunner's tumbler trembled in his hand. Himmler smiled. 'To Kersten's long life.'

~

Irmgard had taken the children for the day. Kersten was at the table eating the scones Elizabeth had cooked when he heard the doorbell rang. He rose and went to the door. He still had a dab of whipped cream on the corner of his mouth.

A stranger was standing on his doorstep looking miserable and frightened.

'Yes, can I help you?' Kersten asked. It was an overcast day and birds were twittering in the trees about.

'My name is Miss Hanna von Mattenhein. I'm a friend of Karl Veyzel, your patient. We did meet once, you and me. I was at Karl's house. I left while you were on the way out. We passed briefly and smiled at each other.'

Kersten searched his mind. Futilely. 'How is Karl?' Kersten finally asked.

'Well that is why I'm here.'

Kersten stood aside as she entered the foyer and removed her wide brimmed hat that Kersten received and put on the stand beside the door.

'Would you like some tea or coffee?'

'No,' Hanna replied as they moved into the lounge where they sat.

'Water then?'

'Maybe later.'

'So what is wrong with Karl? If he is sick he knows to contact me.'

'He's not sick I'm afraid.'

'Not sick I'm afraid.' Kersten said perplexed. 'Then what is it?'

'The Gestapo have arrested him. They think he's an agent.'

'Oh God.'

Hanna lowered her eyes. When she lifted them she was smiling.

'You have a piece of cream on your mouth, Mr Kersten.'

If it was one thing Kersten had learnt it was how quickly he had to act to save people. The following day he visited Brandt he had come to love as a dear friend. Himmler's little, self-effacing secretary didn't disappoint him. He retrieved a file from his cabinet. He handed it to Kersten who took it with the type of solemness that he took the file on the Dutch deportation all those years ago. Once more Kersten sat as he did then, hunched over a paper that trembled in his hands. As then, the truth of the words crushed him. When he looked up at Brandt his face was pale. 'So it's true old Brandt. My friend really is a spy.'

Brandt shook his head gravelly. 'Ay, I'm afraid so.'

The next day Kersten found Himmler sporting a black eye. While Himmler removed his shirt Kersten saw several bruises on the Reichsführer's inadequate torso.

'How did this happen, Reichsführer?'

In the turmoil of embarrassment, Himmler lowered his eyes and spoke quietly. 'I injured myself skiing.'

So he still hasn't improved, Kersten thought with a smile, while Himmler lay down on the couch.

'It wasn't my fault this time. An owl flew into my face.'

Kersten began kneading Himmler's war ravaged body.

'Please, release Karl. I ask you not only as your doctor, but as Felix Kersten.'

'You really have the worst possible friends.'

'How about you Reichsführer?'

'Oh well, you still have some that are alright.'

CHAPTER 39

Kersten made another flight to Stockholm where he met Gunther.

'We must act soon 'Gunther said from his office desk. 'The Swedish government and the International Red Cross will provide the food and transport. But this offer cannot last forever.'

Kersten rubbed the stubbled chin. In between him and success stood the man Himmler hailed a God. 'I need more time. That's all. I can convince Himmler. You must believe me.'

Gunther shook his head, reluctantly. 'Very well.'

Kersten's mood heightened two days later when he met his family at the airport. He wrapped his bear like arms around Irmgard and felt her heart beating against his, and he wondered, not for the first time, how the sacrifices he made were jeopardising the people he loved most.

His happiness, however, was so fleeting, he almost regretted it. Himmler called him. 'You must return.'

~

While on board the plane Kersten thought about the Swedish ships full of food and the German soldiers who were stopping the Swiss from unloading it. Kersten knew the dimensions of his request. He felt like he was heading into the biggest challenge of his life. His mother told him once that people don't change, especially men. Even after so many successes with Himmler, he remembered his mother's words that he never imagined could have meant so much. She wouldn't have known either.

Kersten did not go directly to Himmler. Instead he returned to Hartzwalde where Elizabeth as usual had news for him. They spoke over coffee at the kitchen table. So much was changing. What Elizabeth said disgusted her. He saw it by the contortions in her face. Soon he shared that disgust. Nietzsche , who was one of Hitler's favourite philosophers, claimed there are limits to man's love. Was there a limit to his malevolence and selfishness? Sometimes, Kersten thought not.

'SS all over Switzerland are offering to sell Jews from 500 francs per head to 2,000 for important ones. It's disgusting.'

'They are barbarians in sophisticated times.'

'Tell me, what is Himmler like?'

'He's thoughtful, simple, plain and hardworking. He prefers moderation to indulgence, although he does like one glass of wine after his dinner which he has with a cigar. He says his greatest wish is to die poor, a dream he wants to share with his men. He is also indecisive. Sometimes I think there are two men inside Himmler.'

'You said something once to Irmgard who told me. He's superstitious isn't he?'

Kersten leant forward with a smile and the chair creaked beneath his bulk. 'Do you remember how he invited me for dinner?'

'And he stopped to talk with that blonde boy in the street?'

'That's right. Well when I arrived to his home, we sat at his round table. He told me no more than twelve people were around to sit at it, as was the case with King Arthur.'

Elizabeth laughed. Kersten thought about Himmler's round table, his dedicated and almost austere lifestyle, his fondness for women and children, and how he preached loyal obedience and poverty to his men. Was he not, in some strange way an evil Don Quixote? He preached archaic notions like, "the heroism of the sword", and 'heroism of toil'. Himmler desired the path of knight errantry that demanded toilsome difficulty, bloodshed and impoverishment. A path that subjected all who took it with hunger, thirst and discomfort. Like the mad errant, he worked through most of the night and suffered physically for his exhaustive workload and his fantastical imagination. The Jews were perhaps his windmills.

As requested, Kersten accompanied Himmler on the SS train bound to the western headquarters in Berchtesgarden. The iron wheels turned with a jolting, screeching motion across the tracks that glistened in the raw day. They passed green fields that inspired Goebbels's propaganda campaigns: movies and posters showing Aryan women and children playing in fields of clover and farmers pushing their ploughs through earth. Sunflowers dotted the leas, and Kersten realised how innocent and reluctant nature remained while men travelled across the world to slay each other. Kersten looked at Himmler beside him, reading his book. Why wasn't he admiring the beautiful country outside their window, the land he mythologised in his strange, long winded sermons?

The hours passed. Finally, Himmler put down his book and rubbed his eyes that were always red from reading. Like all high ranking Nazis, Himmler often worked himself to the point of exhaustion.

'I've freed the Danes and Norwegians. We'll see about the Dutch.'

'You can do one more thing to confirm your glory. Switzerland is ready to take 20,000 Jews from the concentration camps.'

Himmler gazed up at the mountains where Hitler was staying. 'That's hard, very hard. Anything to do with Jews is hard.'

No one said anything for a long time. Himmler picked his book up, but he only read half way down the page before he put it down again beside him, clasping his hands between his thighs. He looked intently into Kersten's face. 'Let me tell you a story, Kersten.' Himmler finally said.

'Look at those mountains. Right before Germany invaded Poland, Albert Speer saw the usually pale green Aurora Borealis turn deep red over that mountain where Hitler retreats. As a child the Führer survived while four of his siblings perished. In the First World War he was eating in a trench when someone called to him. He rose, walked twenty meters, sat and resumed eating as though nothing strange had happened. Later he discovered a shell had exploded over the trench he had just left. Every member sitting there had died. Months later he escaped a bullet by eighteen inches that killed his friend. To my knowledge he has survived no less than nine assassination attempts and a car accident. Now you tell me, what type of man is that...'

CHAPTER 40

'Come Kersten, listen.' Elizabeth called to Kersten who came into the kitchen where he found his housekeeper with her chair pulled up in front of the radio. It was early morning. The broadcaster spoke loudly, quickly, urgently.

'Finland has asked Russia form armistice and has broken off diplomatic relations with Germany. Ambassador Kivimaki is under house arrest.'

Kersten rose and went to the phone and called Brandt. The voice at the end sounded tired.

'Don't worry. They were Himmler's exact words. He told me to tell you that.'

Kersten drove quickly to Molchow to see Kivimaki. It was only fifteen miles away. They had been relocated there after The Finnish Embassy in Berlin had been bombed. Kivimaki met him looking surprisingly well. 'I'm glad you've come. Now I'm interned to Germany and stuck here like the turd on a bottom of your shoe. How are you?'

'I'm managing alright. As long at Himmler's stomach cramps abide my family and I survive. His health is wretched right now, actually. I'm surprised he hasn't contacted me today already.'

But Himmler had summoned Kersten. Elizabeth told him so when he came home.

On September 1944 Himmler's private train transported him to Field Headquarters codenamed Hochwald where he spent so much time. Kersten walked into the Reichsführer's office that was tastefully but simply furnished. This was common to all Himmler's bureaus.

Kersten entered Himmler's room. He was wrapped in his bed sheets, turning over with great pain. The Koran sat at his bedside.

'You Finns are a fine lot. You're just a bunch of traitors.'

Kersten bowed his head. This time, he would have to hear Himmler out. The Reichsführer worked himself into frenzy so bad he held his twisting stomach. A pulsing vane stood out on his brow like a cord about to snap. Sweat was running down his face, into his small, grey eyes. His face was waxy with pain, an ashy colour. 'Don't just sit there like a log,' he yelled spraying saliva. 'Help me. I can't stand it for Christ sake. It's killing me.'

So it was again that Himmler's pain defeated even his rage. Kersten alone could free him of his grief. A grief that twisted him from inside out. As long as Himmler retained his power this pain would follow him as would Kersten. Kersten knew that.

'Is your family well?' Himmler asked, flat on his stomach, as though he were being weighed down by his suffering that flattened him like a boulder.

'Yes, thank you.' Kersten replied, welcoming back Himmler's good twin. 'I no longer have the right to treat you.'

'Politics have never come between us and they never will, my dear Kersten.'

'Then you won't prosecute the three hundred Finnish families here who have no interest in politics.'

Himmler closed his eyes. 'I promise.'

'One more thing. I may need to contact you from abroad.'

'I can't believe I haven't told you. You need to call 145. When you ring ask for 145 first. Then give the specific number you want. You'll have any connection you want in less than twenty minutes. You go and visit your Swedish leaders.'

Himmler still sensed Kersten's brooding air.

'There is something else, isn't there?'

'Karl Veyzel. You will spare him?'

'You have my word.'

Kersten had no reason to doubt Himmler. The Reichsführer had never disappointed him before.

'My family and I must retain our visas to enter and leave the country.'

'So be it.' Himmler said with a wave of his hand, as though he was a tired emperor allowing an insignificant subject to have their way. 'I hope you're satisfied. Russia will slaughter the Finns. For you can't expect that any will survive.'

Kersten celebrated his newest success with a trip to a restaurant with his family where they ate pork ribs. After his second glass of soft drink, Kersten excused himself and pulled himself away from the table. 'I must go to the toilet.' Irmgard who was laughing with her sons barely noticed.

Kersten pushed open the door, walked up to the urinal ad unzipped his pants. He pissed and while he did so a man spoke to him from the next urinal. He was a friend of one of his patients, a man Kersten had met several times and who was a renowned Christian.

'I'm sorry about your friend, Karl.'

Kersten frowned. A toilet flushed and a man walked out from a lavatory isle and began washing his hands.

'What do you mean?'

The religious waited until the stranger had dried his hands and left.

'The Gestapo hanged him.'

Kersten eyes widened. He felt like he was dying. Everything sounded muted as though he were listening to the outside world from the bottom of a well.

CHAPTER 41

On the eight of December 1944 Kersten arrived at SS headquarters without an appointment. He mounted the stairs squeezing his cane angrily. He burst into Himmler's office. The Reichsführer lifted his eyes.

'You promised….'

'Dear Kersten, please…'

Kersten did not wait to hear Himmler explain himself. How could he trust Himmler ever again? He slammed the door behind him. Brandt seized his arm. 'He had no choice. You saw the files. Hitler made him do it.'

Kersten began to breathe more freely. He ran his hand around the brim of his fedora. Himmler looked sorrowful when he knew Kersten had discovered the execution. That was true. This gave him another idea. 'You're right, Brandt.' Kersten patted the little man's arm and returned to Himmler's office. He removed a note from his trench coat.

'I need you to free 3,000 Dutch, French, Belgian and Polish women as soon as possible to Sweden. I need the immediate freedom of 450 Norwegian students and 50 Danish policemen.'

'I'd like to see them die. But since you're half Dutch, all right I agree.'

'I want 20,000 Jews. Sweden will shelter them.'

Himmler went pale. 'Hitler would hang me on the spot.' His voice trembled with terror.

'You have the power over your men to keep it secret.'

Himmler quickly pulled himself together. 'All right.' he said leaning with both hands spread wide on his desk. 'But all I can give you is two thousand, at most 3,000 Jews. I beg you not to ask more.'

The Reichsführer then seized his stomach. 'I'm in great pain.'

Kersten treated him.

Kersten knew he had to act quickly. The Gestapo would be latently hostile towards these actions and they'd make sure the wheels of bureaucratic process turned slowly. Himmler could change his mind at any moment.

'I want to go home for Christmas and spend it with my family.' Kersten told Himmler during a therapy session.

'Of course. The only thing I ask if that you call me as often as possible.'

Kersten returned home to Hartzwalde to pack his bags. His Christmas family holiday was an excuse to hide his real intentions: a visit to Gunter. Kersten was in his bedroom sorting his underwear when Elizabeth came in.

'A letter,' she said. Kersten opened it and read it. The Reichsführer had given Kersten a Christmas present: the lives of three Swedish men wanted for espionage that were to be executed.

'Dear Kersten, this will be my Christmas present to you. Take these men with you in your airplane.'

On the twenty second of December, 1944, Kersten met the three Swedes who boarded the plane with him. The mood of these men was both joyous and grave. Surreal. While climbing the steel steps to the cabin one of them told Kersten words he never forgot: 'This is surely the best Christmas gift someone can receive.'

Kersten met him with open arms and pats on the back. They were now like two old friends. Gunther had strong coffee sent to them along with chocolate cake that Kersten heartily ate over a China plate. It was good to be out of the Black Forest that was so gloomy. Christmas brought with it an enchanting winter, the sound of glasses clanging and logs crackling in fireplaces. Snow fell in the streets and outside windows. Children pounded each with it. But even amidst these festivities great work was to be done.

'Himmler informs the Swedish Government that it may contact the Gestapo in order to regroup the Scandinavian prisoners into one camp.' Kersten said wiping his chin. 'It has complete freedom to organise the transportation of these souls. The Reichsführer has already ordered his men to co-operate fully with Swedish representatives.'

'You've done a tremendous job. I will inform the government at the next ministers' conference. I'm sure they will receive the news favourably,. I shall see you in the new year.'

Kersten leant back in his chair chomping the last of his cake with a look of satisfaction in his blue eyes. Things, however, were not going so well for Germany. The Third Reich's death rattle resounded loudly like a church bell tolling. Allied armies would soon be crossing bridges they had built over the Rhine. Russians were pouring from Poland into Romania, Hungary, Austria and East Prussia. A new dilemma faced Kersten. What would the Nazis do with the concentration camps? It was their character to punish scapegoats for their misfortunes in the most barbaric ways. They were also conscious of the allies discovering their war crimes. If they panicked they would try to bury the evidence. Kersten knew that the death camps couldn't have been a complete mystery. The Allies planes must have photographed the camps when gathering information. They had to know to some extent what was happening.

CHAPTER 42

1945 arrived. Kersten returned to see Gunther, this time at the diplomat's house. A servant nodded Kersten inside where Gunter was waiting for him. They walked into the lounge room where Kersten noticed two new modernist paintings adorning Gunther's wall. He paced before them, absent yet thoughtful, observing the faces dunked with garish, swirling colours.

'My new year's resolution is to spend more time and money on the things that give me pleasure. One of them being art.'

Kersten studied them close up with his hands behind his back. He ran his eyes over the violent and strange shapes and patterns. 'The Führer hates abstract art. He would sterilise this artist.'

'Oh,' Gunther said pouring himself a Scotch. Kersten quickly glanced behind him as he heard the liquid fall into the crystal tumblers. *The news must be good*, he thought.

'Hitler was a failed painter, wasn't he?' Gunther continued. He never offered Kersten a drink. The doctor had told him he had only let alcohol pass his lips once. That was when he had drunk Cognac after British bullets had almost taken off his head on the plane bound to Munich.

'Hitler only had 'moderate talent.' Gunther said smelling his glass. Imagine if he succeeded. Then we wouldn't have had this absurd and terrible war.'

'Perhaps.' Kersten said folding his hands in his lap. For a moment, Gunther studied those hands which had done more than seemed possible. 'The Swedish government has decided to gather the buses that will transport the prisoners from Germany. You're hard work has paid off, Kersten.'

'My only regret is that I haven't been able to save more.'

Kersten had one more hurdle to cross, even though he was confident he could cross it easily. He knew Himmler was a man of his word. But even he had lied when he hung Karl who he promised to spare to Kersten.

'You have my approval, Kersten.' Himmler said over the phone. 'I've chosen a place for the grouping.' This was better than Kersten had expected. 'The camp Neuergamme near Hamburg will serve your needs perfectly.'

A month of negotiations between Germany and Sweden transpired. Kersten spent a time eating and pacing around. He felt useless. For the moment, affairs were out of his hands. He was a mere bystander. Finally on the fifth of February, Kersten's phone rang. He knew just by listening to it ring that it was Gunther.

'Count Bernadotte, vice president of the Red Cross is responsible for the fleet of buses. Before he proceeds he must meet the Reichsführer to discuss technical details. He wants your word that the Gestapo will treat him respectfully. Will you introduce Bernadotte to Himmler?'

Everything, it seemed, was falling into place. Kersten had heard of Bernadotte. He was closely related to the Swedish royal family. Kersten rang Himmler's office.

'He's not here.' Brandt said. Kersten told the secretary about the convoy of buses that would drive so many prisoners out of the camp gates.

'I'm so glad your plan is coming through at last.' Brandt said.

'Our plan you mean. I owe you so much, Brandt. While history will remember tyrants like Hitler it will forget people like us. Most may even throw us into the same waste baskets as the Nazis. But our children shall know and their children will know after that, the good we have done. '

On the nineteenth of February, Folke Bernadotte's plane touched down in Berlin. He emerged looking about with his long, noble and serious face.

The Swedish ambassador introduced him to Kaltenbrunner who was gloomy as usual. He shook Bernadotte's hand reluctantly with an open hand. The men then sat and talked. Schellenberg noticed something unbelievable. Kaltenbrunner was taking a shine to the count. The discussion went as smoothly as business transactions between two titans can. The count thought he had inspired what little imagination Kaltenbrunner possessed. When Bernadotte rose to leave he shook Kaltenbrunner's hand again, except this time the handshake was true.

'I will praise the way you handed our discussion with the Reichsführer.' Bernadotte said proudly. 'He must realise you are a fine soldier, a real asset to Germany.'

Kaltenbrunner's eyes lit up.

The count's visit to Ribbentrop was less successful and even more painful. The foreign minister leapt out his seat and shook Bernadotte by both hands. Ribbentrop had heavy lidded graceful eyes that made him look sleepy. They were close together that made him appear untrustworthy. Bernadotte was amused to find someone almost as dull as Kaltenbrunner. Bernadotte could not flatter this man who ate into their time with long winded dialogues of how the allies risked Bolshevism if they did not side with Germany. He raised his fist and ranted as though he were impersonating his Führer. The count nodded his head to this tripe. He had to go through a lot of trouble to meet with this Himmler who bore crimes so terrible on his shoulders no deed, including this one, could exonerate him.

His meeting with Himmler eventually came. Himmler promised the

Red Cross busses would take the prisoners to the camp at Neuergamme, from where Sweden would receive them. Despite the good impression the count had made on him. Schellenberg worried that Kaltenbrunner would come between the buses and the prisoners.

'This is a present to Kersten.' Himmler said to the count, near the closing of the meeting as he showed Bernadotte the door. 'Their freedom they owe to him. Not me.'

CHAPTER 43

Theresienstadt was a concentration camp in Czechoslovakia. Fortress Terazin, as it had been called, was built in the 1700's to hold military and political prisoners. The Gestapo, under Reinhard Heydrich's command, had turned it into a ghetto, surrounding it with a large wall which prisoners sometimes mused upon, wondering of the world outside they knew they would never see again. The camp was a sorting and a re-distribution centre where Jewish underwear and garments passed through the hands of toiling workers. Others made coffins and sprayed military uniforms with a white dye to provide camouflage for German soldiers on the Russian front. Yet the Nazi's portrayed Theresienstadt not as a concentration camp, but as a serene Jewish settlement. Benyamin, an inmate, was impressed by how well the Nazis had created this façade.

On June 1944 the Nazis permitted the Red Cross to visit. Karl Rahm sent many prisoners away leading up to that date to overcome crowding in the crude barracks which held more people than seemed possible. The prisoners built fake cafes and shops. They painted rooms that held only three people in each. Old women on their knees with rags and bucket scrubbed clean the walls and the stone ground outside the stores. Old men chased the rats away with brooms. Rahm met the eight Red Cross representatives with a smile and a handshake. He took three of them under his arm and led them into the 'settlement village.' 'This evening, I have a special treat for you,' he said with a wink, his serious and handsome face shining.

After a long tour of the beautifully painted cafés, shops and sleeping quarters, everyone gathered in a long hall as the stars dotted the sky over the fortress roof. The wooden chairs were not the most comfortable, but everyone soon forgot about that when the Jewish children appeared on the stage in make-up and costumes to perform an opera, Bundibar, written by an inmate Hans Krasa. It was a great success. The sweet faced kids sang with all that their hearts knowing soon they would all be dead. When the opera ended, the children lined up at the edge of the stage holding each other hands aloft as they bowed over their tiny polished shoes before stretching high as they could. The audience lifted themselves from their seats and clapped wildly.

The Nazis wanted to repeat the success of this operation. To do so Karl Rahm called the famous actor, Kurt Gerron, into his office. He had appeared in The Blue Angel opposite Marlene Dietrich. He had fled to France where he and his wife were captured before being sent here.

'We want you to make a film which shows the neutral continents how well we treat our inmates.'

Kurt had told Benyamin this. He said how Karl wanted him to show how the Reich 'protected' the Jews. This infuriated Kurt. He knew how his friends had frozen and starved to death behind these fortress walls alone. 'But what can I do, Benyamin?' Benyamin nodded. He blinked his blind eyes, glazed over like sour milk, and squeezed Karl's hand. They were inside the barracks where it was safest to speak. 'You must do what you can.' Benyamin patted Kurt's hand. 'God looks after the rest.'

Kurt nodded. 'Then why does the Yiddish book say faith is childish and trust is vain.'

Benyamin laughed and ruffled the young man's hair. 'You either think too much or talk too much.'

A silence passed between them. Benyamin knew this place made a Prometheus of men. It made of them also the vulture that fed on their liver. Thinking too much was not good for you here. No room for sentiment. Only simple pleasures. Like the sun that felt good on their shoulders, on their upturned faces. Kurt frowned at Benyamin who grimaced as he bent over holding his side. 'I don't feel so good.'

'Are you in pain? Is it your heart?'

'No, no.' Benyamin said, fending Kurt gently away with his hand. 'Just a stomach ache. It's the food, that's all.'

This was no place to fall sick and they both knew it. People who fell ill ended up as smoke in the crematorium chimneys. It amazed Kurt how this old man could still elude death.

The old man took a few pained breaths. He seemed better. 'Remember when you first came here and you told me who you were, and how you worked with my favourite actress.'

'Yes…'

'Well you still haven't given me your autograph. I've been waiting for years now.'

Kurt laughed heartily and threw his arm around Benyamin. 'It would be no good to you my friend. You couldn't see it.'

Rahm had his way. Kurt shot 'Terezin: a documentary film of the Jewish Resettlement,' He was happy to have somewhere to channel his energy, although to enjoy it he needed to forget the purpose of the film. The Nazis would hopefully appreciate Kurt and his colleague's efforts to conceal the camp's true nature. They used all their skill to create a replica world, a virtual universe opposite to the real one. The commanders would respect Kurt's artistry and that of his helpers and spare them. After all, the war was going to end soon. Surely, the Germans wanted to make a good impression and free their prisoners.

On January the 26th 1944, the cameras and microphones came out of storage where they had been gathering dust. Kurt and his wife rose from their hard wooden bunks. They had dreamt the night before of their old lives when they were happy in front of the camera.

Benyamin was bent over a lump of local ore that he was splitting with his chisel and hammer. He excelled in this role and well he should for it literally saved his life. Benyamin ran his hands over the rock, exploring the grains and textures with his fingertips, searching for mica. He must have looked like some strange ancient faith healer with his white, shrivelled eyes and his feeling hands. Once, a guard hovered over him and told him, 'You have miraculous hands.' Benyamin nodded subserviently and thanked the supervisor before chipping away at the stone. Today, however, he was not so careful. He had a strange premonition. Kurt and his wife were heading for trouble. A tragedy was going to unfold. The blind man could not explain it but he saw it. He trembled all over and he struck his hand with the hammer, something he had never done. Benyamin cried sharply and grabbed his hand. A guard rushed over to him and seized his fingers where the blood ran warm and thick. Benyamin barely had breath to speak. 'I'll live.'

The sun had not yet risen when an officer pushed a rifle butt into Benyamin's chest. He opened his blind eyes to the familiar darkness. He smelt Vodka and cigars. Sound of leather boots stomping boards that trembled as though they were also scared. The shadow of several SS officers towered over Benyamin who put up his forearm to shield his contorted face. 'Get ready,' one said.

CHAPTER 44

The officer's metallic voice cut through the morning stillness. Air cold as ice.

'Your train is on its way old man. You must prepare for your special treatment.'

Benyamin tottered out to meet the locomotive. 'Has anyone seen Kurt? I must tell him goodbye.' Benyamin said to Marcel behind him.

'No, he's still making that film, isn't he?'

The mute prisoners huddled together. They were too cold to speak. They had no flesh to stop the chill. Benyamin heard only a few children sobbing as their mothers swept them into their arms. He heard the SS guards hauling open the cattle wagons. They herded the prisoners on board. Inside the carriage the air dissipated with every prisoner who came aboard sucking the air until their lungs hurt for there was none. The guards then hauled the doors shut and bolted them. A whistle cried longer than seemed possible. Wheels began to grind and roll. Moments later the jolts of the train were throwing Benyamin against the bodies that were crushing him. No room. He had never been so thirsty. He listened to the sick wheezing and coughing all day long. Sometimes the children moaned and their mothers whispered to them that they would be alright and that good people were waiting for them. But there were no good people left and everyone knew it.

The train crossed the German border. Benyamin smelt fresh excrement. A woman had died beside him. His breath was faint as though it wasn't his. Benyamin raised his chin. You had to fight for every piece of reeking air. He felt like Tantalus reaching eternally for fruit on a branch that was always just out of reach. A part of him wanted it to end. This part had been with him for a long time.

Time flowed like a dream. He didn't know if he slept or not. Benyamin thought he heard people having oral sex in the darkness but everyone ignored it. He thought of his premonition. Why did he not see his own fate? After all, he was the chosen to die. Everyone knew by now there was no special treatment, unless one broadened that term to include death that was at least release. When he thought about his fate, Benyamin wondered whether his life had been good. What made life worthwhile? Was it love, wealth, success, friendships or laughter? Perhaps, it was simply peace and contentment. Most likely, it was all of these things. Benyamin had experienced them all, but he still wasn't ready to die. No one here was. The world would probably say his people didn't fight hard enough. But they had. They had kept themselves alive, and that was the biggest fight of all.

Benyamin felt sorriest for the children and the young people who had barely had a life at all. What could they say about their lives? No sooner had their time begun and they were thrown into concentration camps, and made to suffer worse than animals. At least the Nazis were honest. They said the Jews were lower than animals and that is how they treated them.

At last, the carriage screeched to a halt. Moments passed before the guards wrenched open the carriage doors. They immediately put their arms over their coughing mouths to stifle the stench of human waste, sickness and death. Sunlight burst in. The prisoners lifted their sinewy hands to the heavens to shield their eyes. The soldiers waved them out and they descended slowly for they were no more than skeletons. When they left the carriage the soldiers did not hit them with the butts of their rifles. Nor did they seize them or scream in their faces like they usually did. They simply stood silently to one side as though making a guard of honour, watching the prisoners hobble between them. Some fell but their friends helped them back onto their feet. Everyone smelt grass and dirt. No stench of burning flesh. A strange feeling overcame them. It was difficult to recognise because they had not felt it for so long. But it didn't take them long to realise what it was, for the sensation was natural as love or hate, happiness or sadness. It was freedom.

The inmates moved meekly as beaten dogs. Benyamin wondered how these skeletons bore the blows of the SS batons. It defied physics.

It hurt the prisoners to raise their heads, because they were sick and starving, but when they did they saw there were no executioners waiting for them. They did not believe it at first. The Red Cross nurses were smiling at them, some of them weeping as they took the broken people in their arms and held them.

Brandt put down the phone. He looked at Himmler who was fussing at his desk over papers. 'It's done, Herr Himmler.' Brandt said as though he didn't trust what he was saying. Himmler kept his head lowered as he spoke. 'Well when the head of the convoy rang me to ask my permission I heard that number, 2,700 Jews. It took me only a moment to realise why that number meant anything. Kersten, I thought. It was just enough to satisfy the good doctor's wish.'

When Himmler looked up, he was smiling.

CHAPTER 45

Kersten was sleeping when he heard a knock at his apartment door. He was still in Stockholm. He sat up and slung his feet over the bed and into his slippers. He yawned and glanced at the clock on the wall that read 2.31 pm. Kersten had indulged in one of his large lunches and had been feeling tired ever since.

'I'm getting too old for this,' Kersten muttered to himself as he made his way to the door where someone knocked again.

'Alright, alright, I'm coming.' Kersten said. Mr. Von Knierin, a banker and friend of Kersten's was standing at the door.

'Hello Von. Come in. I need a coffee. Would you like one?'

'I was hoping you'd say that.'

Kersten sat hunched over his coffee, cradling it on the table with both hands. His Batlic Russian friend observed him from under his thick grey eyebrows that shaded his black eyes. He had a plain and serious face that seemed to hang from his gaunt cheekbones. 'This is more than a social visit, although I am glad to see you.'

Kersten laughed. 'I rarely receive them these days.'

'Well, war is big business. I come on behalf of the World Jewish Congress. Stockholm's representative of this organisation is Hillel Storch. He wants to see you.'

Kersten smiled. 'It seems like I'm getting a reputation.'

'You're becoming a legend.'

Hillel was short with a big nose and wore heavy rimmed glasses that along with his fuzzy hair made him look intellectual. Kersten met Hillel in the ambassador's office. Hillel was nervous and smoked a lot. Not a moment passed when the man didn't have a cigarette dangling from his fingertips. He studied Kersten through blue fog. He looked like a man at the end of his rope, kept alive by nervous tension, by blind defiance of despair that had sucked everything else from him.

'I've heard so much about Mr. Kersten. You are our last hope. Can you help my people?'

'Give me a memorandum stating what the World Jewish Congress wants. I'll do all I can as soon as I return to Germany.'

Kersten went home to pack. He would return to Berlin. He no longer had his Eastern headquarters in Zhitomir in the heart of Ukraine. His new base was only twenty five kilometres from Hartzwalde. Soon Kersten would once more be standing before the Reichsführer, pleading for mercy. First, however, he had to visit Gunther.

~

Himmler always became nervous when he talked to his Führer, even if it was only over the phone.

'Can you carry out this task, Himmler? I cannot bear the army's incompetency any longer.'

'I promise, my Führer, I shall not disappoint you. I shall blow up every concentration camp. No Jew shall walk free as long as I am head of SS.'

'Good, good. I know I can trust you, Himmler. You would never betray me, would you?'

'My Führer, I owe everything to you. I would give anything for you. You know that do you not?'

'We must blow up the camps soon.'

'Give me the order, Führer, and I shall obey.'

Kersten threw his large case on the bed and began stuffing it with documents. Then he packed his personals, starting with his rather large underpants when Hillel burst in waving a telegram above his balding head. He looked breathless and red faced like a drowning man signalling for help to someone on the shore. If he looked dead when Kersten saw him last than he looked worse than that now. Kersten expected bad news. And so it was.

'They're going to blow up the concentration camps.' Hillel said, his neurotic, finicky face going awry. 'No Jew will escape. We must intervene before it's too late.'

Gunther met Kersten who was trying to stay calm. They sat in the diplomat's office. Kersten told him about the news Hillel had brought. Gunter said he knew about it.

'It is horrible. The Americans want us to stop it, but how does one converse with Hitler. He's mad. And he's getting worse.'

Gunther leant forward and spoke in his smooth, intelligent voice to Kersten who listened carefully, writing down everything the Swede proposed.

'Firstly, we must stop the detonation of the camps. Secondly, we must-'

'Just wait a moment. Okay. Go on.'

'Secondly, we must do something about Kaltenbrunner who is holding up Bernadotte from evacuating Swedish prisoners. '

Kersten lifted his head and read out what he had written so far. Then Gunther continued. 'Thirdly, we want you to convince Himmler to order German troops in Norway to surrender, fully armed for the allies are pressuring us to take arms against them.'

Kersten sighed and rubbed his head. He had so much to do and so little time to do it.

Germany seemed poised for defeat. But this seemed to have only strengthened their resolve to kill more Jews. The death trains continued to puff steam and showers kept flowing. Bodies kept piling up and the men that enforced these murders descended into craziness beyond knowing. The smoke from the crematoriums in Auschwitz soared like never before as though a dragon had woken.

The railway tracks that led to Treblinka revealed new horrors. Bodies lay in their excrement beside the rails, growing in number the closer gates drew. The emancipated corpses were twisted, their upturned eyes staring at the sky. Maggots nestled to sleep in their rotting bodies, and the black birds pecked at them and squabbled, flapping their wings outstretched like capes over the heads of the dead. The smell of flesh wafted so strong on the breeze it was unbearable. Yet the guards seemed immune to it, or otherwise, half-crazy if they had not been already. They sat drunk around the fires that lashed spitefully, drinking from bottles of liquor with prostitutes on their laps. Although it was cold, some men were naked wearing only their boots and breeches as they drunk themselves into stupors, wheezing and drooling like lip jerking idiots. One sat on a dead child palms down on their knees looking about the forest. Water stood in pools on the soft earth churned up by boots, cattle and tyres. A stray dog sniffed at the puddles. Some soldiers squatted and shat before all to see. Then they rose up without wiping themselves, pulling their clothes about them. They glanced at immense trees that soared fifty feet into the air. When they had finished drinking and eating the deer and fish they had killed the soldiers crouched in silence watching the fire, their greasy faces shining. Some slept off the meal, lying down to sleep among the dead. They snored with their greasy mouths open, while flies crawled over their faces. They woke when the moon rose, sitting on the edge of the forest. The general stamped his feet and flared his arms like a wild bird and the bats fled in confusion. The general then lowered his sweat mattered balding head to continue drinking. He paused only to leer at his Jew girl, no older than twelve, with a collar around her throat. A delicate thing chained to a tree, naked, trying to cover herself as she cowered in the dirt. The flames lit up his eyes and his teeth as he studied her, his mouth foaming. What beast had this war woken in such broken men?

Piles of cherished valuables, stolen from their Jewish victims laid scattered; money, gold, silver, objects that passed through the hands of thieves now heaped in the dirt, where they somehow retained their beauty, and indeed were more innocent and beautiful in a world that had lost both of these things.

~

Himmler's new office had once housed dying soldiers. It was pitiful. Yellow paint was peeling from the walls revealing the raw masonry beneath. Kersten felt as though he were standing in Himmler's frail mind that resisted the world falling down around it. The room was bare, cold and crude. A light bulb burned and fluttered in the ceiling as though it too was dying. Himmler was sick. Only his perverse optimism saved him from the terrible truth.

'Nothing is lost,' he told Kersten, perspiring with pain. 'We have new weapons, even better than the V2.'

Kersten said no word and treated him. Soon the Reichsführer's body relaxed as his spasms subsided.

'Is it true Hitler ordered you to blow up the concentration camps when the Allies approach?'

'It is. Who told you?'

'The Swedes.'

'It doesn't matter that they know. If we lose the war, our enemies will die with us.'

'The great German leaders of the past would not have acted like that. You can stop it. You have your SS. You are more powerful than Hitler. Be generous.'

Kersten was summoning the knight errant inside Himmler's imagination that lusted for everlasting renown and fame. But Himmler, who sought this renown while lacking the necessary courage, said nothing.

'I ask you to stop Kaltenbrunner from holding up Bernadotte's convoy.'

'I can't believe he's being insubordinate. You will have your white buses. I promise.'

'What about the camps. Do you promise not to blow them up?'

'I cannot promise that. Hitler gave me a direct order. You ask too much my friend. I will never do it...I cannot.'

Kersten's shoulders slumped under the weight of his woes. There seemed nothing he could say to Himmler to make him change his mind. This wasn't the first time he had encountered such an obstacle. Years ago he had begged Himmler to save the lives of a Jewish family who had been detained in a concentration camp. After months of effort, his pleas came to nothing. But Kersten would not give up.

The next day Kersten returned to Himmler's pitiful little office. He tried again to convince Himmler to cease the bloodshed but the Reichsführer shook his head. 'I will not,' he said, looking vicious and serious. Kersten shrugged. A week passed like this. All Himmler had left was his power to drag people into the grave with him. Kersten, however, also had a power: the power of his hands. He used this power to take the bad blood away from Himmler's heart, replacing it with invigorated and healthy plasma. Sometimes, it was enough to put Himmler into some transcendental state. *Where does he go*, Kersten wondered? The Reichsführer lifted his sweaty head as though he were surfacing from the sea. 'I shall do as you ask.'

Kersten and Brandt gathered around Himmler who lowered himself before his crude wooden table. The bulb burned above them, casting their hunched shadows over the peeling walls. Himmler looked like a withered tree bent in a storm. How weak he had become. A cigar in the corner of his teeth. He'd never smoked like this before. He badly needed a shave. His uniform hung from him like dying leaves.

Nothing like this will ever happen again, Kersten thought. Not in the war or in all of history. Minutes later Himmler finished the agreement which stated no concentration camps would be dynamited and that white flags would be raised above them when allies approached. Jews were to be treated like normal prisoners, and no more would be executed. After Himmler signed it he gave it to Kersten to sign.

'I'm going to lie down,' Himmler said lowering his bloodshot eyes, as though this momentous deed had taken away the last of him.

CHAPTER 46

Kersten continued treating Himmler at the old convalescent hospital. When he visited he smelt death; not death of an individual but of something much greater. The Reich no doubt, Kersten thought. It would never see its proclaimed thousand years. Hitler was delusional like Himmler. No one can take over the world. Hitler's exquisite intuition served him too well. If he had suffered more in the beginning than the greatest bloodbath in history could have been avoided. He may have even saved his demise. He could assign all the fresh faced little boys he wanted to take up arms but it would do no good. The Reich had reached the summit of its tragic grandeur and was now capitulating. In Hague, this was evident as it was everywhere. The German's had turned Clingendael into a virtual fortress. But Clingendael's beautiful gardens and winding tracks and its 400,000 would not save it. Hitler gave liaison officer Fegelien the order to blow it up with the V-2. Fegelien rang through the order to Himmler who could hear the artillery exploding in the background. Himmler liked and favoured the young man and had been present when Fegelien had married Eva Braun's sister, Greti in a simple but elegant ceremony. That was before the war began to wear on Fegelien who had begun drinking heavily despite his pregnant wife. Fegelien, who even now sounded slightly intoxicated, relayed Hitler's order verbatim: 'This city of Germanic traitors must die before us, and to the last man.'

Himmler informed Brandt who waited until he had a spare moment to notify Kersten who was home helping make dinner when he heard. Kersten broke out in a sweat and his cheek seemed to stick to the phone that he put down gently, to avoid alarming Irmgard.

'I've got to leave...' he told his wife who looked at him, tied into her apron.

'But...'

'I have no time. Keep my dinner warm in the oven.'

Kersten sped away in his car over the gravel tracks. He narrowly missed a three legged dog that he had to swerve to avoid at the last moment, almost rolling his car. He'd seen the hound wandering around a few times before. He didn't know who owned it, if anyone.

Kersten shook his head and went on. When he reached Himmler's headquarters the first stars were blinking in the cold sky. In Holland the light of the V-2s would join these celestial bodies. Except, unlike stars they would not recede into blackness. They would plunge into the earth and they would take to their graves the lives of innocent people. A city reduced to a mushroom of ash and dust drifting into the sky as though it were a soul rising from the slaughter.

SS guards stood darkly against the sky. Brandt met the doctor at Himmler's door. He had already drawn up a memorandum on the capitulation of the German army in Norway which he handed to Kersten who swept it up as he flung open the door to Himmler's office. He planted the paper down on Himmler's desk. The Reichsführer studied it from behind his spectacles. 'The city is Germanic. I shall spare it.'

Kersten, panting, sank into a crude wooden chair that barely supported his weight. He stretched his long legs wide apart, and mopped the sweat from his forehead with the back of his arm. He smiled at Brandt who leaned in the doorway, neither in nor out.

That night Kersten did not sleep well. He remembered the promise he had made to Hillel. This would be the hardest task of all. worshipped Hitler like a God, and he hated Jews and felt as though he had been ordained to destroy them. The Führer had personally assigned him with this burdensome but meaningful mission. How could Kersten change that? That he could entertain the thought, gave him hope. After all, no one, not even Kaltenbrunner could deny, how important Kersten had become to the Reichsführer. Maybe, on some strange level, important as Hitler. He could not rely on Himmler's signed document although it was a good start. He needed to assure himself and the world that Jewish prisoners would board the Swiss buses.

Irmgard turned over in her sleep, and muttered something in her dream. Kersten blinked at the ceiling. Tomorrow he would ask the impossible. He would ask Himmler, the man who had killed more Jews at once than any other person in history, if he would sit face to face with a representative from the World Jewish Congress to discuss the lives he had promised to save.

~

There was rain in the wind. But Kersten didn't bother with an umbrella as he approached SS Headquarters where he began treatment on Himmler.

'What would you do if a representative of The Jewish World Congress visited you to arrange for the liberation of the Jews which you promised me?'

Kersten spoke casually. He felt Himmler's body twist.

'You're crazy. You expect the second man in the Reich to meet with their greatest enemy. You've finally lost it, Kersten.'

'This has nothing to do with enemies and foes. Imagine how the world will accept you if they discover you've freed Jews.'

Himmler hesitated. 'Do you think so?'

'Sure.'

'But how could I do that without Hitler finding out.'

Kersten tapped Himmler's flabby stomach. 'You'll find a way. That is why you're the genius leader that the world will remember. And it will certainly remember this intelligent and courageous act, Herr Reichsführer.'

Kersten was running out of time for negotiations. Tomorrow he had to visit Sweden. He told Himmler this when he finished the days treatment. Himmler sat up and ran his hand around the back of his neck that he jerked from side to side.

'Tell the World Jewish Congress I will see their representative. He will have a pass and I promise no harm will come to him. I ask only one condition: he must come with you.'

'Where shall we meet?'

Himmler didn't speak. He had no idea.

'Hartzwalde.' Kersten suggested. 'And Brandt and Schellenberg shall be witnesses.'

'As you wish.'

CHAPTER 47

All night Kersten laid awake wondering why Himmler had turned his back on what had both made him and destroyed him. Was he trying to exonerate himself in the eternal eyes of history? Was he hoping the world would forgive him because of this small act of belated mercy? Kersten took these thoughts with him all the way to Stockholm where he met Gunther in the diplomat's office.

'I have news.' Kersten said, lowering himself into the chair. He sat his fedora in his lap and ran his hand around its brim. 'The German army in Norway will surrender, and the concentration camps must raise their white flag when the Allies arrive. Not one shall be dynamited. Himmler gives you his word.'

Gunther studied the man before him. *What makes this chubby masseur so special*, he thought? He was good natured and intelligent, but how could a simple therapist achieve so much?

'There is one more thing.' Kersten continued. 'Himmler said he will meet me and a representative of the World Jewish Congress.'

Gunter leant back in his seat. 'The biggest Jew killer in history has agreed to meet a Jew. That's not funny, Kersten, not even in peace time.'

'I'm not joking.'

'Thank you. From the bottom of my heart. Your good work will be rewarded. But now you must leave. You're jokes are not funny. The Jewish congress won't think so either.'

'You'll see.'

Kersten rose to his feet and shook Gunther's hand. The diplomat did not blink. He stood staring at Kersten. 'You're serious aren't you?'

'See you later, Gunther. As always, it has been a pleasure.'

Kersten screwed his fedora over his large head, twitched his imaginary moustache and walked out the door swinging his cane, whistling, as though he was that crazy Jewish comedian: Charlie Chaplain.

Kersten arranged for Hillel Storch to visit him.

'Sit down, Hillel. I have something to tell you.'

Hillel obliged. They were in Kersten's apartment. He poured Hillel a strong coffee and one for himself before leaning back folding his hands across his girth.

'I have a message for you. Himmler invites you for coffee. Like we're doing now. Although, I imagine it may be a little tenser.'

'I would be grateful if you did not joke. This subject is too serious and painful.'

'But I'm not joking.'

'Then this war has driven you crazy. It doesn't surprise me. I can't imagine hanging around Nazis all day would be good for your brain.'

'Do I look crazy?'

'Why are you doing this, Kersten? You were meant to be helping my people.'

'I thought that is what I was doing...'

Hillel pulled his ear and turned away. 'At least Hitler keeps his promises.'

Hillel rose to leave. Kersten held up his palm to stop him. 'Very well,' Kersten said drumming his paunch with his fingers, 'Let me show you.' Kersten stood up and straightened his trousers. 'Well...come on.'

'We're we going? Is this another trick?'

'I'm going to call Himmler.'

'No'

'Why not? Don't you think the Reichsführer has a phone? C'mon man, there are lives counting on us. We have no time for cat and mouse.'

Kersten was put through to Himmler's office. But as soon as the Reichsführer began speaking with Himmler, Hillel took Kersten by surprise and left. Kersten apologised, hung up the phone and chased after his contact. He was half way down the staircase when Kersten leant over the bannister. 'Come back. Please. I beg you.'

Hillel halted, as though he had woken from a dream. He craned his neck and gazed at Kersten. Reluctantly, he trudged slowly up the staircase, one slow step at a time. Kersten was holding the door open for him. Kersten took him by the shoulders and looked him straight in the eye.

'This is difficult to believe, I know. But I have known this man for five years. I am the only person in the world who has been able to relieve his pain. This has allowed me to wield great persuasion. What we are dealing with is a subservient personality. Someone who would follow his Führer to hell and back if the Führer so wanted it. Maybe, in some strange way, I have taken a similar, albeit smaller part in this man's life. You must believe me.'

Hillel looked into Kersten's blue eyes. They had taken on that savage, penetrating glare again. It was the same look he had when he refused his friend Rosterg's offer to treat Himmler before the war.

Hillel nodded towards the phone. Kersten didn't have to say anything. He dialled again and received Himmler's direct line, after giving the special number Führer had given him: 145.

'Herr Himmler, it's Kersten. I am here with the Jewish representative. I'm afraid he thinks I'm full of horse shit. Did you not agree to meet him for coffee?'

Kersten held up the phone so they both could clearly Himmler's high voice.

'Yes, Herr Kersten. Now when are you coming back?'

Hillel shook his head. He had heard the devil admit it. He could not believe it, but reality told him otherwise. The next day, Hillel cabled New York to ask permission to the World Jewish Congress to visit Heinrich Himmler, head of the Gestapo and overseer of the Reich's concentration camps. Hillel did not have to wait long for the message: 'Do it.'

CHAPTER 48

Kersten had packed his bags and arranged them at the door. He was drinking coffee in his apartment when he received a disappointing phone call. It was Hillel. 'I cannot go.'

'What do you mean? The plane leaves in three hours. This may be the last chance.'

'So many of my family members have died in concentration camps. The Swedish government cannot grant me a passport. But I have arranged someone to take my place.'

'Who?'

'Norbert Masur. He's a Swedish citizen and practicing Jew.'

Kersten glanced at his wristwatch and rang Masur. He wanted to make sure the man had prepared to go through with this. The voice at the end of the line sounded calm and intelligent. 'I'll do whatever it takes to help the Jewish people.'

Kersten contacted Himmler.

'It makes no difference,' the Reichsführer said.

'He has no visa.'

'No matter. As long as he as he is with you. I warn you not to contact the Foreign Embassy because Ribbentrop will find out.'

Kersten arrived at the airport on April the 19th where one of the last airplanes to bear a huge Swastika waited. Kersten glanced at his wristwatch. The plane was due to take off in minutes; at two pm. Masur was nowhere to be seen. Storm clouds gathered. He paced around before looking up when he saw a tall, dark young man with an intelligent, handsome face. 'Sorry I'm late.'

Both men understood the surrealism and gravity of this mission. These thoughts consumed them. During the flight neither spoke. They were the sole passengers. Kersten sat with his hands crossed on his stomach and his eyes barely open. The roar of plane's motor pounded their ears. Masur saw little sign of war save for a bomb crater in a field. The strange calm of the fields below seemed without end. Yet this was only the calm prelude to the storm. Once they reached Berlin this would all change.

Four hours later, they touched down to a deserted Tempelhof where only a few policemen on duty wandered about like lost souls. It was dusk. They greeted the two flyers with a Nazi salute. Masur removed his hat, and in his most polite voice said: 'Good evening.'

Kersten handed over his visa to one of them. He swallowed hard and glanced at Masur beside him. Himmler had kept his word. The young man was allowed to pass.

The car that should have been waiting for them wasn't there. They waited in a small room overlooking the tarmac. It had faded yellow walls and linoleum floors. Kersten sat watching a fly crawl the wall. Masur looked outside the widow. There was nobody there but them. They felt tense. When they heard the speaker crackle to life, they stiffened. Goebbels spoke. Masur and Kersten glanced at each other. This had to be important.

'German people, rejoice. Tomorrow, the twentieth of April, is your beloved Führer's birthday.'

The two men felt more surreal than ever. The German people were starving and dying as bombs fell in their cities and towns leaving smoke solid as stone, while Russian soldiers left a trail of rape and murder as they poured across the borders. Such a birthday message seemed ironic amid this suffering. It came from Hitler's bunker.

CHAPTER 49

The message ended and a car marked with the SS insignia on its black, polished doors pulled up. A secretary came out and handed Kersten and Masur two conduct passes that would substitute for visas. They were both signed by SS Brigadeführer Schellenberg.

Soon the car rolled into Berlin. The shadows had grown long in the streets. A red sky. Refugees marched along the roads dragging suitcases, some crying with their hands to their faces. Women yelled at their ragged children to hurry. Some pushed prams full of loot, liquor, jewellery, whatever they could find, fleeing like carnival freaks and snake oil sellers chased from a village.

Masur put his face to the window to stare at the scars the Russian, English and American bombers had left. 'Oh God,' he whispered.

The chauffer wanted to drive fast to miss the bombs but he could not because rabble was blocking his path. Masur desired to be noble and mourn this destruction. But he was so furious with Germany, that part of him enjoyed the ruin. Schadenfreude.

Armoured cars made narrow pathways through the fallen remains. Some of the buildings looked like a giant had bitten them in half. Decapitated towers scorched black. Brown water lying through streets. Factories without roofs where trunks of sunlight spread along the desecrated floors. Ruined houses reared up, and in between the rubble and shadows, camouflaged tanks leered out like sleeking predators. Several female civilians shambled over the bricks, wrapped in their fur coats they would not leave behind for the allies to steal. Darkness fell early and the bombs would not be far behind.

All trip long Masur thought about his relatives who the Germans had dragged off these streets and sent away to the death camps. He turned to Kersten.

'This will be the most improbable meeting of the war.'

The SS car had only just reached the open road when an officer stepped from the shadows and raised his palm. The chauffer wound down his window as the soldier bent over. 'Turn off your headlights.' The air-raid alarm rang through the din. The driver lifted his head and gazed up at the searchlights bearing his throat as he swallowed. The bellies of planes passed overheard. The thunder of their engines took Masur's breath. The sound of distant explosions echoed as planes dropped bombs like burning dragon eggs. Piercing fires soared in all directions. Clouds of grey smoke. A low boom. Masur heard his window rattle. Something vast and formidable had woken.

Masur watched the flames on the horizon beneath the shelter of a tree on the outskirts of the city where the chauffeur had stopped. They looked like scattered torches burning against the sky. The hill trembled beneath him as though an angry God was rising from the dead. When Kersten closed his eyes, the bombs sounded much louder in the darkness. At midnight, the driver pulled up on the gravel driveway at Hartzwalde. The doctor gave Elizabeth Lube the coffee, tea and cakes he brought from Stockholm. He wanted to greet his guests with class. He had to make sure everybody, especially Himmler, were happy.

Kersten had heard nothing from Himmler. While Masur sat in the lounge room, Kersten paced up and down by the front window. It was already two am. The morning lay long before them. The clock hands circled endlessly. Kersten could barely breathe for the stress. Masur felt too surreal to feel anything. But he remained calm. Headlights finally appeared through the lace curtains. It was Schellenberg. He was tired, anxious and afraid. He spoke to Kersten in a hushed but urgent voice. 'I have little faith in this meeting. Hitler's last wish is to take his enemies with him. Bormann shares this desire. Himmler fears Martin and is jealous of his closeness with the Führer. I believe Himmler will give in. He's gone far not too, hasn't he?'

Schellenberg and Kersten watched each other silently, reading in the other's face their dismay.

The animals slept in their barns and the stars pulsed quietly. The Jehovah Witnesses were snoring in their outhouses. A cool wind rustled the grass. Elizabeth looked even more tired and disappointed than Kersten. She seemed unaware of how dejected she looked and sounded. 'You've done all you can,' she told Kersten, squeezing his shoulder. She had never seen Kersten so weak and fatigued. His eyes looked raw, his mouth tight, compressed, defeated. She leant on the chair cupping her forehead.

Kersten poked the logs crackling in the fireplace. Tiny specs of fire scurried into the darkness. Kersten stood before them, thinking. What had happened to Himmler? Perhaps one of the Allie bombs had buried him on his way here. Hitler may have given him an urgent mission. Maybe someone had arrested him. Kersten was sitting with lowered eyes when he heard a car pull up in front of the steps. A polished leather boot emerged from the black car, preceding a high peaked officer's cap with a silver deaths-head. Himmler was dressed in his best uniform weighed down by many medals, including an iron cross glimmering over his heart. Brass buttons on his double-breasted topcoat. He had just come from the Führer's birthday 57th party.

Masur ran to the window to peek. Kersten strolled outside. Schellenberg followed. Brandt stood beside the Reichsführer. Kersten could not make out the look on Himmler's face beneath the brim of his hat.

'Sorry we're late, Herr Kersten.' Himmler said, raising his head at last. 'The allied planes were flying over us at treetop height, firing at troops and dropping bombs. It was as horrible as it sounds. More than once, we had to throw ourselves into ditches.'

Himmler's suit looked spotless. But Kersten didn't question the Reichsführer. Instead he spoke to him in his reassuring, almost angelic voice that had calmed the Reichsführer from the day they met. 'Thank you for keeping your promise. You must be friendly to Masur. The world is shocked by the way the Third Reich has treated its prisoners. This is your last chance to show that Germany has changed, and is humane.'

'You can depend on me to bury the hatchet.' Himmler said. 'If I had my own way, many things would have been done differently. But I've already explained to you how things developed with us and also what the attitude was of the Jews and of people abroad.'

Kersten led Himmler inside.

Kersten felt like he was nearing the edge of a waterfall. He took Himmler where Masur waited. The Reichsführer's high boots rang smartly on the boards.

'Reichsführer Himmler....Mr Norbert Masur, representative of the World Jewish Congress. '

The two men bowed to each other slightly.

'I am glad you have come.' Himmler said.

'Thank you.' Masur said.

The two men sat down in silence. The millions of dead souls sacrificed to the gas chambers seemed to shatter the air between them.

'It is good to see you again.' Himmler said. Kersten raised his eyebrows. He glanced anxiously at Masur, wondering how the young man would react.

'You don't know me.' Masur said.

'Oh but I do. We've known each other since time began.'

Himmler's tone was cold and ominous. Elizabeth came in with a tray of coffee, tea and cakes that she placed on the table. Masur had tea, Himmler coffee. Elizabeth returned with plates of jam, butter and honey along with brown bread. Himmler removed his glasses and wiped them clean with his skull embroidered handkerchief.

'You know all about me, don't you Mr Masur?'

Masur nodded to show he did.

'Men of my generation never knew peace.' Himmler said putting his spectacles back on. He stirred his coffee deliberately and slowly. 'I hold the Jews responsible for they controlled the media, capital, and the governments-the world's lifeblood. All of which they've diseased with their filth.'

Men like Hitler love war like other men love women, Masur thought in scornful silence.

'The Jews fired on my men in the ghetto. They resisted us, and carried typhus that they planned to use against us. And for cremating enemies like this the Allies threaten to hang us!'

Himmler turned pale with passion. 'Concentration camps! Huh, they should be called education camps. Thanks to them, German had her lowest crime rate in 41. The prisoners worked hard. But all Germans do. That is our way. Maybe it is not theirs. Oh well...'

Masur could no longer restrain himself. 'But your men committed crimes in those camps. If beating and killing people is education then you can keep it.'

Himmler turned his head slightly, as though he were trying to see something from another point of view.

'Maybe at times our men were excessive...'

'Let's break for some fresh air, shall we.' Kersten said. 'Here, have some coffee.'

Kersten poured Himmler a cup which he graciously accepted. While he drank it he didn't remove his eyes from Masur for a second. Himmler finished his cake and wiped his mouth on a napkin. He remained calm and superficially friendly.

Kersten took Masur outside and whispered in his ear. 'Hang in there. Just remember what is at stake.'

Masur nodded. 'Everyone needs an enemy.'

When everyone returned the mood was more peaceful. Kersten wanted to keep it that way. 'Let's not talk about the past. We cannot change that. We must talk about the future.'

Masur, like Kersten, moved and spoke with more clarity and focus. Like someone who was resolved. 'I want you to assure me that all the Jews who still remain in Germany will keep their lives. Only then can we build a bridge between our peoples of the future.'

Himmler said nothing. Everyone glanced at each other. Then Himmler spoke in a reflective voice. 'Heydrich and I planned a town inhabited exclusively by Jews, who also administered it themselves and managed all the work. We had hoped that one day all camps would be like that.'

'Let's go through the list of people from the Swedish Foreign Office who we want to release.' Kersten said.

'Yes.' Himmler replied. 'But let us do this alone, shall we.'

'Of course.' Schellenberg said, tapping Masur's shoulder as the two men left Kersten, Brandt and Himmler alone.

'I will fix the figure at a thousand.' Himmler said. 'But there will be more.'

Himmler had one fear: that he would be uncovered. He was afraid of Hitler, even now, as the dictator hid in his bunker beneath the pounding assaults of missiles that were destroying Berlin. But a shadow of the ruler he had been, shaking uncontrollably, obsessing futilely over his maps, the ceiling lights trembling with the motion of falling bombs.

The clock ticked away. The fire roared quietly. Finally, Himmler leant forward and signed a paper that would authorise the freeing of one thousand Jews to leave Ravensbruck. Himmler paused half way through and lifted his pen. 'These Jewish women must be recorded as Polish, not Jewish.'

Masur nodded. Himmler proceeded. No sound except for the clock and the ink running across the paper. The clock read five am. Himmler threw down the pen, leant back and rubbed his eyes. Then he rose to his feet. 'Goodbye, Masur,' he said and left the room with Kersten.

Schellenberg was desperate to leave with Himmler. They wanted to go to Hitler's bunker to put an end to his power so they could begin peace negotiations with the Allies. Brandt stayed behind at Hartwalde. He thought it was too late. Germany was in ruins. The Reich was finished. Forever.

It was dawn when Himmler emerged outside with Kersten. It seemed the sun had risen early to witness this strange event and sombre parting.

The shapes of trees, mountains and fields began shaping themselves in the new light. Himmler opened his car door and stood waving to the doctor. Then he paused. 'On second thought save as many Jews as you can. What does a few thousand matter now?'

Himmler climbed into the back of his Mercedes and lifted his dull grey eyes.

'We wanted greatness and security for Germany and we're leaving behind us a pile of ruins, a falling world. Our good intentions have destroyed us.'

Himmler hesitated as though to brace himself for the gravity of his next words. Or perhaps he was simply wheeling internally about those he had just spoken. 'History will try to pervert all the good things I've done for Germany. Those who are left to govern this country hold no interest for us. The Allies can do what they like with it.'

The Reichsführer shook his head. 'I owe you everything, Kersten.' He took the doctor's hand and squeezed it. His eyes welled. 'My thoughts now rest with my poor family. Farewell.'

The motor started and the car disappeared into the gloom.

~

The officers burst through the barrack doors. The air was cold. The women raised their heads in blackness. Their eyes were dark and pale in their sockets. Sweat stood on their brows.

'Up,' the guards yelled. They rarely used more words than necessary. The women swung their bony legs over the side of the bunks and touched their feet on the cold boards. Their knees trembled. The guards prodded them with rifles and told them to hurry. The door opened on its groaning hinges. They came out of the moon on their thin haunches. The SS arranged them into groups of five. They huddled together wrapping their rags around their sunken shoulders and the top of their spines protruded through their pale flesh. Somewhere a dog howled. They heard their breaths. They shuffled in their stinking shoes, shrinking against the cold, the guards beside them. They looked ahead. As though there was anything there. They went on along the barracks in the mud. The gates opened slowly. They stood beside the guards who were hollow, without inner reality. Outside the iron doors the white buses waited white as angels. A red cross had been painted on them. The people inside were dressed in white and they came out and they took the prisoners in their arms and the prisoners cried.

CHAPTER 50

Kersten ate his last meal at Hartzwalde. Elizabeth came in and sat beside him. Brandt was still sleeping. He and Schellenberg had agreed to raise the number of Jews that would be rescued from the camps. They would also prevent the circulation of any final desperate orders, such as indiscriminate shooting of Jews and other prisoners at the approach of the Allies. The destruction to German communications made this last objective easily possible. Orders supressed in the throats of wires. Lives saved.

The logs on the fireplace were ashes. As soon as Kersten thought he was gaining a second wind, his tired eyes began to flutter slowly beneath the crushing weight of fatigue. But he would not rest until he was on the plane that could not fly him fast enough from this fallen city. 'So the Jehovah Witnesses will stay and look after the animals,' he said. 'They don't have to.'

'The Nazis took their assets and the Allies bombed their homes. They have nowhere else to go.'

'How I know that feeling.'

A pause.

'It is no longer safe for me here.' Kersten sighed. 'The Russians consider me guilty by association.'

The Russian tanks would roll in and they would spare no mercy. Kersten was Himmler's doctor and they would treat him as such. They would hang him and his family from the tallest tree. That was one reason why Kersten had decided long ago to move to Sweden.

'You were a soldier in the Finnish army weren't you.'

'I still have a photo of me in uniform as a young man. I'm taking it with me in my shoebox. Himmler was right about one thing.' Kersten paused to ponder. 'We've never known peace. There will always be war. It may not be fought with canons, airplanes and machine guns. But man shall always fight each other. And even I, a man of peace cannot see men changing.'

Kersten and Elizabeth thought about their future. This felt more like an end than a beginning.

'I have only 450 Swedish crowns and I'm almost fifty. I have three young boys to bring up. Yet I am happy. The worse is over, Lube.'

'Yes,' she replied, reaching across the kitchen table to squeeze his hand. All of a sudden, Kersten felt that this need not be an end at all. It could be a beginning.

Kersten packed only one large suitcase. On the way out he halted before a mirror on the wall. He felt like he was looking at a stranger, someone much older that he barely recognised. Even his brilliant blue eyes looked paler.

With their travel passes signed by Himmler, Kersten and Masur waved farewell to Brandt and Elizabeth who stood waving from the front step. The two conspirers drove through Berlin. For Kersten, it would almost be definitely for the last time. The city looked like an asteroid had hit it. A corpse of a great animal left rotting in dust and grey light.

The car went slowly past the devastation. Vagabonds in rags wheeled wooden carts heaped with mountains of loot that they strapped with rope. They were covered with dust as though they had merged with the ruin they shambled through. Young boys threw stones at each other across the fallen bricks and pretended to shoot machine guns. One stumbled back as imaginary bullets ripped him to shreds. He fell with his tongue lolling from his mouth. *War is in us*, Kersten thought. *It will not end. It will go on. Forever.*

Tempelhof was deserted. It seemed to hold its breath, as though it were waiting for Kersten who stepped out of the car. A raindrop spat on his fedora. He paused to listen to the Russian artillery exploding in the distance. Death lingered. He was so close to it he could smell it. The cool wind carried it for miles. The mind would carry it forever.

The propellers spun and the motor roared like an angry mosquito. Soon the plane gained altitude over the broken city, churning up the clouds. He watched Berlin growing smaller until it looked like it could fit in his hat. Never to see it again. Kersten leant back and closed his eyes. So tired. He looked forward to seeing his family. He felt calmer than he had done for a long time. He crossed his hands over his stomach and dreamt of an auspicious future.

CHAPTER 51

Fifteen motely men reached Neuhaus and parted in three different directions like a something torn apart by some great wind.

Among this group were Sergeant Heinrich Hitzinger and his towering aides: Werner Grothmann and Heinz Macher who both dressed as army privates. Macher was barely more than a boy but he was a highly decorated Waffen-SS captain Hitzinger trusted.

They walked for many miles until they reached the streets of Bremervorde that would take them to the bridge at Bremervorde in the North. In their tired imaginations they could already hear the running water. Sweet as music. They longed to scoop it in their hands and drink it on their knees for they had walked long and were thirsty. They longed to splash it over their skulls and faces for they were scorching. The future looked promising. They would sleep under trees and inside barns, using their tattered jumpers for pillows. They would wash their clothes in the river and dry them by fires. The men would wake from happy dreams with their backs against the rocks. They would drink the blood of grapes. And when the moon rose they would eat, drink and reminisce by great fireplaces in Falstaffian inns with mountain men big as giants. Hitzinger would feel young again.

The tallest two wore long, dark green overcoats with felt collars. Hitzinger shuffled between these men, wearing mismatching clothes under a blue overcoat. He looked dishevelled and unwell. That he was in charge gave the trio's appearance a touch of the comic, for he looked no more than a puppy dog struggling to keep up with its owners.

In the West the sun was touching the ground. A brief flare. Soon night would come. Darkness would follow the starving refugees, forced labourers and German soldiers on crutches. So many of them had come so far. Those that did not make it hung dead from trees, their bloody chins sunk into their chests like saints in prayer. The SS had left them dangling beside roads for others to see what would come of them if they chose 'defeatism.'

People fled, nevertheless. In great hordes. All tired and black with dust.

A Scots man, one of the Black Watchman, put an outstretched hand in Grothmann's chest to stop him. The three men lifted their eyes with outrage. Why should they be picked out amidst so many?

The three men were filthy and stank. They looked like dim herdsmen coming up out of the sun. More guards swamped them and the Germans handed over their identifications. The smallest of them, the one with the eye patch gave the watchman a pay book that the officer studied silently for many moments. Then he raised his eyes. 'Sergeant Heinrich Hitzinger. You and your fellow officers are under arrest.'

They were lead to a truck and hauled inside it. They were taken to a mill where Sergeant Baisebrown interrogated them. Heinrich sat crouched on his heels. The men claimed to be sergeants but their smudged SD stamps on their papers said otherwise. Still, they could hardly be important people in any case. The SD forgers had been fooling the Bank of England for years. How could high ranking men mess up something so simple this badly?

The three Germans watched night fall over the mill where they slept soundly. Early in the morning a truck arrived to take them to camp. They blinked like dazed birds in the raw morning light while they climbed inside the trailer. The truck took them far across the countryside. They were weary. Hitzinger regarded everything with disinterested contempt.

The sun shone meekly when Hitzinger and his escorts arrived at camp Kolkhargen, west of village Barnstedt. Karl Kaufmann, the ex Gauleiter of Hamburg noticed the man in breeches, military boots and a civilian coat. The new arrival seemed familiar. He was different from the others, although Karl wasn't sure why.

As though he wanted to prove his oddness, the man disappeared behind a bush and when he reappeared he had replaced his eye patch for rimless spectacles. Kauffman stood with his mouth open. 'It cannot be…'

The three men requested to see camp leader, Captain Selvester, who granted them this wish.

Finally, their appointment came at Selvester's office. A cold evening. The earth's axis was receding quickly from the sun. Hitzinger looked pale and unwell, and in far lesser shape than his strapping friends. He tottered inside. He looked up only once before entering the barracks, to see the dry lightning severing the clouds. Hitzinger had been a superstitious man for all of his life. He took this as a sign. An omen. He had prayed to the Gods in his languishing thoughts. Now they had spoken.

The sergeant and his aides were separated and put in cells with no windows, where the light was dull and raw. British officers interrogated them over a crude wooden table. None of their stories matched. The interrogators took an impressive magnifying glass from Hitzinger, but paid little mind to the eagle wings on it.

When Hitzinger entered Sergeant Selvester's office he did so solemnly. He sat down quietly and glanced up at the captain. 'You don't know who I am.'

'No,' the sergeant replied.

Slowly, the prisoner removed the patch from his left eye, reached into his jacket and put on his glasses. Selvester now knew who the captive really was. He trembled excitedly. The prisoner spoke quietly. 'I'm Heinrich

Himmler.'

Selvester studied this captive. He reached for the phone on the table to call Chief of Intelligence, Colonel Murphy. For the whole while he did not remove his eyes from his silent prisoner. 'I have someone who claims to be Heinrich Himmler.'

'Send him in.'

Selvester threw Himmler a British battle-dress to wear. Himmler, who was pulling on his white socks raised his eyes, and looked at the costume scornfully. 'I would sooner die than wear a British uniform.'

'Who knows? You may get your wish.'

Himmler sneered.

Selvester planted his hands on his hips. 'Then you'll go naked.'

An officer entered the chamber and wrapped a grey blanket around Himmler. They walked him outside to the waiting jeep. Himmler grasped the blanket tight around his shoulders. A cheap stage actor playing the part of a Roman emperor clutching his toga. Himmler kept his eyes lowered over his white socks.

The jeep began its journey. Himmler jostled woodenly between two officers pressed firmly against him. Pine trees reared up around him. The moon followed them between the branches. The wandering German citizens Himmler extolled paid no notice to the mock emperor. They seemed dazed by the odd beauty of destruction left by Allied bombs.

Wind rattled the remains of buildings. It would be a cold winter. The Reichsführer glanced at the world numbly, slouched in his blanket, his white socks sticking out from beneath.

The jeep stopped abruptly, jerking on its springs. Himmler looked about. He was at 31a Uelzenerstrasse, a red-brick suburban villa dressed with ivy. The British Intelligence officers had turned it into an interrogation den.

The officers hustled Himmler up the steps and into the villa. They pushed him into an ornately furnished parlour filled with British officers who stopped to stare. He passed through them with his head bowed.

Soon Himmler was standing before Colonel Murphy. He raised his voice with spite, spitting his words. 'I am Heinrich Himmler. I demand to see Eisenhower.'

Doctor Captain Clement Wells was out of town organising for his home leave and he did not hear the speakers blare out the request for a medical officer to report to police headquarters. When he returned to Ulzenerstrasse, he stepped out of his jeep and noticed how chilly it was. A 'blisteringly cold evening,' he would later recall, 'with a sharp Eastern wind.' Pine trees were tossing their heads frantically. He noticed more sentries than usual, but thought little of it.

Wells was not the regular doctor and he wasn't happy to discover he was being summoned. Sergeant Austin was grinning from ear to ear in the doorway. 'Guess who the prisoner is waiting for your examination.'

Wells shook his head. 'Who?'

Austin, the childish bastard, wouldn't tell him.

Sergeant Major Austin and Dr C.J.L Wells entered the room in house 31a. Wells saw the deplorable man before him almost tripping over the blanket he dragged about his feet.

A guard with a tommy gun along with eight others led Himmler into the next room. A chandelier with a grand shade threw its light over a round oak table. Brocade curtains hung from the windows and beside them a still-life of sunflowers hung from the wall.

Hans Prutzman had killed himself in this very room. Everyone knew Himmler could be carrying a poison phial in his mouth.

'This isn't the end, you know.' Himmler roared. 'Freedom fighters, the Reich's werewolves are gathering legions as we speak. We will have Russia yet. One day the West will bend on their knees and thank us for saving them from Bolshevism. I am here as their leader to offer you peace before it's too late.'

Himmler glared at Sergeant Major Edward Austin who handed him a sheet of paper. 'Sign it.' Himmler obliged, but before the ink dried he snatched it back and ripped it to shreds, letting the pieces fall to his white socks. Himmler looked determined and arrogant as though he knew something no one else did.

'He does not know who I am.' Himmler said staring at Austin.

'Oh, yes I do.' Austin replied in German. 'You're Himmler, but that's still your bed. Get undressed.'

Himmler sunk on the couch, unbuttoning his shirt. He did not take his eyes off Austin. Wells stood holding a torch. 'Open your mouth'.

The sergeant held the light high so he could better see inside Himmler's mouth. He saw a small, black knob protruding through a gap in Himmler's teeth on the bottom right side.

'Get up and come closer to the light.'

Wells was about to put his fingers in Himmler's mouth to remove the glass phial of potassium cyanide when the prisoner jerked his head to the side. Wells cried in pain and fell. Himmler flicked the phial out with his tongue and bit down on it. He collapsed to the ground in agony, shrivelling up like paper in a fire. Austin and Murphy held his feet while Wells gripped Himmler's throat. Himmler's eyes rolled up into his skull.

Wells would not give up. He returned to Himmler's side with a bowl of water in which he dunked his handkerchief that he used to mop the prisoner's mouth. Wells heard footsteps. Officer Whittaker came running down the stairs. Wells sat by in despair, still as the corpse before him that seemed to be sleeping. Whittaker hoisted Himmler up by the ankles to drain the poison out of the dying man's heart.

Two officers burst in when they heard the drama. One held a fire bucket with water. They seized Himmler's ankles and dowsed his head in and out of water. A strange, macabre baptism. His head lolled backward and forwards. Water dripped from the end of his nose and mattered hair.

Nurses bustled in with a stomach pump and knelt at Himmler's side. They dunked Himmler's head into the water until fifteen minutes passed. The red faced nurses sat in puddles of water, surrounded by buckets and swabs. Heads bowed in solemn defeat. The smell of prussic acid spread through the room and the silent corridors. Wells glanced at the clock arms snapping on the wall. 'Time of death: 11.14 pm 23 of May.'

The next morning came bringing with it new tasks for the army at Ulzenerstrasse. Officers Brown, Atkins and Bond hauled Himmler's waxy corpse closer to the window to get better light. They examined and measured him with intense scrutiny, going as far to record the amount of hairs in his ears.

Colonel Murphy held a press conference that same afternoon. He did not meet the press in a room, but in a nearby alley. He led them up and down the street, talking excitedly as though he were on Benzedrine.

The press eventually saw Himmler's corpse, although they could not enter the room to see it closer. Rex North of the Daily Express and counter intelligence officer Neil McDermott stood at other ends of the room eying each other and Himmler's black eye patch and spectacles that sat on a chair near the door. Each man knew what the other was thinking. They made a run for the souvenirs, wrestling each other to the ground knocking over chairs. The guards had to separate them. Both men rose to their feet, catching their breath and straightening their jackets. They smoothed down their hair that stood up on end like cockatoo feathers.

Two days later, Sergeant Major Austin wrapped Himmler's corpse in camouflage netting that he bound with army telephone wire. He tied it tight and was sweating when he was done. He mopped his brow with his sleeve. A strong, young officer helped Sergeant Weston dump the body into a semi- trailer Belford truck. Austin waved his hat to the young officer and sank into a jeep. 'Let's go,' he said. Otto slammed the trailer shut, and Weston sat in the front of the lorry. They followed the jeep driven by Norman Whittaker. It was just after midnight. The truck exhaled exhaust fumes. Weston could just make out the large figure of Austin in the moonlight, a block of pale stone, filling the passenger seat of the jeep.

CHAPTER 52

They drove for a long time looking for a lonely spot. Their quest took them to Luneburg Heath where they began to dig a grave about four feet deep. It was hard work. Whittaker took the jeep to the mess. When he returned he had beers for everyone who accepted them graciously for they were hot and thirsty despite the cold. They stood drinking over their shovels that were sunk into the earth. Officer Otto leaned on his, watching the rain clouds.

Austin brushed a fly away. Wind blew the grass, booming in his ears. Weston clipped open the trailer and the others helped him drag Himmler's corpse into the ditch. They had to reposition the corpse several times because his legs kept sticking out.

'Even an arsehole when he's dead.' Whittaker said in his macho drawl.

The wind blasted the heath, making their eyes water, bending the branches with hellish scorn. Rain began falling into the open grave. The sergeants bent over their shovels and quickly covered the ditch while rain lashed them. They obscured the site with leaves and sticks. Then they all threw their shovels in the trailer, and wiped their hands on their trousers.

Dawn broke over the trees. The officers realised the pit wasn't as conspicuous as they had hoped. 'It'll do,' Whittaker thought.

The officers turned their heads when they heard wild voices muffled in the wind.

A group of drunken Polish soldiers were stumbling up the road, laughing and talking loudly. The officers called them away. Luckily the Poles were too happy for confrontation and moved along.

Silence fell between the American soldiers who stood over the body. Nobody said a prayer for the monster beneath their feet. Austin took a moment to reflect on the type of man he had buried and how God had allowed this life. He prayed for sleet and scum to come dampen this forsaken heath.

The officers dusted off their uniforms and threw their shovels into the back of the truck. They left the heath to wallow in its solemn silence. They wished never to see it again.

When they returned to Ulzenerstrauss a fresh faced reporter in a fedora greeted Austin. The journalist was kneeling on the bottom step with a notepad on his knees.

'I saw the photos of Himmler's body.' the British journalist said standing up. 'When and where will Himmler be buried, Sergeant Major Austin?'

Austin stood straight as a rod, his hands on his hips, his face clouding.

'Nobody will ever know where he is buried.'

But this wasn't entirely true. The grave was deemed vulnerable. Whittaker returned but it took him half an hour to find it. A civilian who happened to be passing by gave them a lesson in reading maps and digging a grave. The officers stood back while he took charge. 'Look,' he said pointing,' the top surface should be kept separate, so you can slide the body right in without disturbing the earth. You do want the grave to be hidden, don't you?'

Whittaker's men chuckled.

It took the officers an hour to dig up the body. Once they had to stop when a German couple walked by with their Dalmatian. The pair was curious enough to pause and look. A corporal yelled at their dog: 'Go onnn, get.' The couple raised their eyebrows and walked on.

Soon another car pulled up. An apathetic man in hunting gear rose out and leant against his mud-splattered car, watching Whittaker and his crew while helping himself to a hip flask. He showed no signs of moving or concern that he may have been interrupting important military business. 'My ride is here,' the civilian said.

A second car appeared later that day. A man holding his back emerged. He wore a black silk scarf high over his pale, shrunken face that wavered in the cold wind behind his gaunt, sunken shoulders. The man looked as though he had been dug up as well.

So this is Germany's fallen hero, Whittaker realised, gaping at the tragic grandeur before him. Only a few signs of this newcomer's vanity remained, notably a soaring pompadour. This was the closes Whittaker had come to mourning the fall of the Reich. For the man hobbling towards him was none other than Walter Schellenberg. The former Brigadeführer had been summoned to identify what remained of his master's body, which he did, nodding gravely, surely anticipating all the while the woes awaiting him at the Nuremberg trial.

~

The American soldiers led the townspeople by force along a muddy track that ran four miles until it reached the gates of Buchenwald camp. The German villagers arrived to the camp still looking smart in their well-cut suits, Sunday dresses and flowered hats to walk among the dead. Some strolled arm in arm. The women wore fine perfume and lifted their garbs when stepping over muddy puddles. The men put grease in their hair and looked handsome. The females buried their faces from the stench with their handkerchiefs as they passed bodies that leered at them. Flies crawled over the gaping mouths of the dead whose necks were thrown back in agony. Trucks and carts loaded to overflowing with gaunt, twisted corpses. The wagons were old and creaked in the heat. Corpses, no more than skin and bone stacked meters high outside ovens like wood to burn. Only days before mountains of them would have would slid down trailers like chaff down a hopper, some with their heads sticking out, others with the soles of their feet protruding. But one day people would pray here and they would bring flowers where the dead had once been summoned.

The troops stood by as the procession filed through the slush. The incinerators opened and the citizens, press and men of foreign power gathered about and murmured. One girl sobbed into her handkerchief. Her makeup ran. Some women hid their eyes in shame.

Nearby, corpses floated face down in the river. Dead children lolling in the gentle current. Who were they? No matter. The people knew the dead are as quickly forgotten as the living are undistinguished..

The Allies pointed at the drifting bodies, and the townspeople fished them out of the currents with branches. Fat women with arms the size of pork knuckles would then haul them up on the banks where they lay dripping. The good citizens would dig graves for the victims of their warlords. The corpses weighed nothing and their last anguished moments embalmed their faces and endured in their upturned eyes.

CHAPTER 53

Menashe arrived at one of Budapest's poorest inner city districts: Jozsefuaros. He had come for miles, across the German border in fact. He followed three black rats that led him through black arches into a courtyard with three stories of flats where his journey would end. He stood in the middle of the square, shrouded in light, beneath his black Jewish wide brimmed hat. He gazed up at the crowded rooms where towels hung drying on the bannisters. Some old people who looked too old to breath stood resting their elbows on the porch wails watching him. A sad grey mist seemed to cloud the air. Children crouched in doorways, unwashed and lice ridden. Hungry eyes that had seen too much woe for so few years. Feet curled up like raven claws. Bony dogs slinking about and dragging their sex between their paws. Menashe saw two of them coupling. An old woman wearing a scarf surfaced from her den and shooed them away with her broom and cursed. Menashe moved on. *What a sad place to end my journey,* Menashe thought. He really did not understand God at all.

Menashe raised his hand and knocked on Benyamin Harari's door.

A tall old man with white, shrivelled eyes tottered out. He wore a kippah that looked new. His robes however, looked like he had found them at the dump.

'Is that you, Daniel?'

'No, it's Menashe. You remember me?'

Benyamin frowned. Then he smiled. 'Come in, friend.' Menashe entered, taking his hat in his hand into the shadows. The door shut behind him. He smelt herbs. Menashe believed you could learn something about a home by how it smelt. This place smelt of someone who was lonely but who defeated their loneliness and boredom by keeping busy. A rug had been pulled over the cracked window like a curtain. Plaster walls were cracked and leaking. An unfinished meal sat on the sink. A bowl of wet cat food going to waste on a sheet of newspaper on the floor. But Menashe saw no cat.

Benyamin shuffled with a limp. Whether this was because of old age, or the legacy of a beating the SS dealt him. Menashe did not know.

'Please, sit.' Benyamin said dusting the couch down with his hand. Menashe sat.

'How are you young man?' Benyamin asked. Menashe was forty, but he hardly looked it, even after spending years in a concentration camp. His voice sounded young too.

'I am well, thank you Benyamin.'

'You sound fit. Can I make you tea?'

Menashe had come a long way. 'Yes, I would like that very much.'

While Benyamin made them tea, Menashe went out for a cigarette. When he returned he found Benyamin waiting for him on the vinyl couch with their tea that he carried in a China jug. His hands were still long and graceful. They had played the piano once. 'In another life' Benyamin once told him.

Menashe poured his cup that he cradled like a bird. He saw Benyamin's nostrils flare.

'Do you still smoke?'

'I quit. But the memories of our days in the camp and the nightmares stress me. I need a crutch. Just don't tell my sister.'

Benyamin threw back his head and laughed. Many teeth were missing in his gaunt head. He still had all his black hair.

'This teapot is the only pretty thing here. Besides me…' Benyamin laughed, nudging his friend.

'You're still sharp as a whip.'

'Aye.'

'And why are you here and not in your home at the other end of town? You used to tell me how nice it was.'

'The Nazis sold it. When I got out of the concentration camp the government told me it was no longer mine.'

Menashe nodded. He had this story many stories.

'My friend Daniel, told me I could stay in this flat. He told me it wasn't much. Well, he wasn't kidding was he?'

They laughed.

'So did Kurt ever finish his movie for the Nazis?' Benyamin asked. Menashe paused. He rested the cup on his saucer.

'He did. The day after that they took his wife and him away on the death train to Auschwitz.'

All Benyamin's humour deserted him. He seemed to shrivel up like he was dying.

'They sent him to the showers. The next day, Himmler stopped the gassing.'

Benyamin's mouth gaped. Everything went still. A dog barked in the distance. A baby cried in the room above them.

'Kurt knew he was going to die. So he told me to give this to you.'

Menashe removed a note from his pocket that he handed to Benyamin, clasping the old man's hand around it, tenderly. He saw a single tear run down the deep lines of Benyamin's face.

'Would you like me to read it to you?' Menashe asked as Benyamin opened his hand.

'I know what it says.' Benyamin said. 'It's that bastard's autograph.'

Menashe laughed and cried. It was true.

'I hounded him for it for years. And now when he's dead, he finally decides to get it to me. Do you believe that?'

CHAPTER 54

The fresh faced clerk looked over his desk at Kersten.

'I'm sorry sir, but you cannot see Mr. Christian Gunther. He no longer works here.'

'Then I would like to see your manager, please.'

Kersten was at the Swedish Embassy. He had come to apply for citizenship. Hitler was dead and the war was over. The Swedes seemed to have already forgotten it had happened. Kersten couldn't believe that people in this office had treated him this way, after what he had done to free their fellow citizens from the concentration camps while providing their government intelligence. He sat in his little wooden chair, stunned, while the clerk returned with his supervisor, a medium sized man of thirty five who wore his slick hair parted to one side.

He leant with his back on the clerk's table and studied Kersten with amusement and even contempt. Kersten could bear it no longer. 'Are you aware of how many of your people I've saved? Now you won't even give me and my family a citizenship.'

'I suggest you visit the Finnish embassy then. You have citizenship for them, don't you?'

Kersten froze and an ironic smile appeared on his lips. 'You seem to know much about me. You should know I cannot move to Finland. The Russian have the country by the throat. It is not safe there...'

Kersten did not raise his voice. But he was beginning to seethe.

'My superiors have advised me to pass you on this message, Mr. Kersten: your presence will be tolerated by the Swedes only if you keep yourself in the background.'

Kersten shook his head in disbelief. Was this a dream? He rose and walked to the door. He turned around and glanced at the secretary and his supervisor. 'I shall return.'

The secretary moved his lips. He didn't speak but Kersten read the man's lips clearly.

'Nazi.'

The secretary smirked. Kersten's heart dropped. He bowed his head beneath his sorrow. He pulled his fedora low on his face, as he left.

Kersten climbed to the stairs in his apartment slowly as though he were sleepwalking. He passed a room where he heard a mother yelling at her child.

When Irmgard saw Kersten come in looking pale, exhausted and drawn, she realised something very serious had happened.

The boys were reading in their rooms. She was boiling soup on the stove. Kersten breathed in the hearty smell of it. He removed his coat and draped it over the top of the couch. Then he slumped down on the vinyl cushions, holding his hands across his stomach, overwhelmed by his thoughts. Irmgard sat beside him, stroking his thinning hair.

'These people treated me like I was the one who had sentenced their people to death, when I put my neck on the line to save them. Why? I don't ask for their flattery. I only want to live my life here and raise my family...'

'We'll be okay.' Irmgard said softly. 'If we survived a world war and the Gestapo we can beat this.'

But Kersten was still obsessing about his misfortune. 'You've heard about Count Bernadotte's book that just came out, haven't you.'

Irmgard lowered her head solemnly.

'I thought so. Well old Delwig has. He told me all about it.'

Kersten turned his face to Irmgard. 'He doesn't mention me. He doesn't mention Gunther or Norbert Masur either.'

Kersten rolled his eyes in his disbelief at the ceiling. 'I didn't want public acclaim like he obviously does. But I needed him to confirm my part in freeing those prisoners to save me from the rumours that say I took part in Himmler's atrocities.'

'It'll be okay. You have-'

'You know what an upstart clerk called me today?'

'No...'

'Nazi.'

Kersten sighed.

Irmgard looked into space. Mute as stone. Kersten glanced up at her. He remembered how pretty she looked the day she drove him to meet Himmler. He hugged her tight to his chest. 'I'm sorry for putting our family through this.'

'Don't ever think that, Kersten. You gave me and the boys that beautiful estate to live in. We lived well while others starved and died. You did brilliantly.'

Kersten seemed calmer. He stared with his wife into the space where their lives seemed to float before them, like a balloon taken by a wind that kept escaping their fingers.

'People forget one thing.' Kersten said thoughtfully. 'I too am a survivor. Did I not cheat death every day when I asked Himmler to spare people from the crematorium? Heydrich was literally a second away from arresting me when Himmler called and saved my life. If I had left a second earlier with Otto I would not have received Schellenberg's message and Kaltenbrunner would have shot us to ribbons. How many of his comrades stood behind these thugs ready to take up their cause and stick a knife into my back? Now not even those I saved want me. They think I'm making everything up to save my fucking arse.'

Kersten slept in late the following morning. He locked his eyes like cages against the light. He was depressed. Outside his flat the world continued. Cars zipped across Stockholm, people met friends and shop doors opened. Money floated through countless hands. Workers invested their energies into an evolving society. People were born and people died.

Taken as one figure, people seemed insignificant with their duplicity. But taken as individuals each one was a mystery with strange tales and sinister secrets. People were often not what they seemed.

Irmgard came in and sat on the end of the bed. 'Get up, you,' she said bouncing on the mattress.

Kersten raised himself on his elbows.

'You have a letter.' Irmgard said handing her husband an envelope. She left him to open it alone.

The typed letter was two pages long. The Jewish World Congress had sent it. They thanked Kersten for saving about 60,000 Jews. Kersten sat on the edge of the bed, his palms pressed into the mattress. Something deep rose from deep within him, like a dark, strange storm and he could not stop it. His blue eyes began to well.

Kersten showered. He sat on the edge of the bed, pulling on his shoes. Irmgard came in holding his letter. 'I've read it three times. You must keep it somewhere safe.'

Irmgard stood thinking, looking about. 'I'll put it up here,' she said opening the wardrobe. 'In your shoebox with your Finnish army photos.'

'Thanks darling.'

'Where are you going?'

'For a walk. Tonight we'll go out for dinner.'

'We don't have much money...'

'We have none. Still, I insist. We've been moping around inside for too long.'

Kersten kissed his wife. His took his cane that he had leant against the wall and put on his fedora that he kept on a hook. He opened the door and turned around to face Irmgard.

'Bernadotte says I was a Nazi collaborator. After all I did.'

Kersten smiled bitterly and shut the door behind him.

CHAPTER 55

Kersten found a discreet, stylish café that sold the type of pastries Delwig and he had eaten years ago. He sat beside the inside window overlooking the street. In the background a gramophone played the Andrew Sister's 'Don't Sit Under The Apple Tree'. He had not heard it before, and he couldn't deny its ironic simplicity and sweet, nostalgic melody lifted his spirits.

Kersten lowered his face into his mug of strong, black coffee and drank heartily, like a beast lowering its fat head into a water hole. *Think positively*, he told himself. He had two appointments next week with old patients. Tomorrow, or even this evening, he would contact his old friend, the Dutch ambassador. Kersten believed the ambassador would inform the Swedish Queen of his sad circumstances. She would hopefully clear his name; a name which his poor children would have to bear long after he had died.

Kersten had almost finished his coffee when he heard people whispering about him in the corner. He glanced at them. They turned away. Kersten swivelled his head back around like an owl, shaking it. He sniffed. When people saw him they did not see a Nazi collaborator. All they saw was a middle-aged fat man.

Kersten paid the shop keeper with a crumpled up note he dug up from his jacket. Then he left feeling poor and lonely.

He sunk his hands into the endless pockets of his trench coat that almost swallowed his forearms. He thought about Himmler's parting words, how despite all good intentions, the Nazis had left behind a country in ruins. Kersten understood clearly what happened everyday: you don't have to kill people with guns and knives. You can do it with ideology.

Kersten's life had come crumbling down with the bricks and mortar of Germany. He had served humanity in the only way possible and yet his lot was in some way cast in with the people who had tried to murder him twice. He was now a ghost. A man without home or sympathy. Alone. For the first time in a long while he wanted to surrender to his self-pity and cry. Something he wanted with all his heart. But he would not. He walked on.

At around two in the afternoon, Kersten chanced upon a book store. He frowned at the front window. The store was displaying signed copies of Count Bernadotte's book, 'Slutet', The End. Some of the books were turned backwards. A photo of Bernadotte in his regal uniform, with chest thrust proudly out, graced the dust sleeve, his intelligent eyes peering at all who passed

Until now, Kersten had avoided the book. Yet he decided he would succumb to his curiosity. He wanted to look at it and get it over and done with.

A bell jingled as he entered. The small store was dim and quiet. Kersten took Bernadotte's book from the shelf and leafed through it. A woman stood beside him. She was also reading the count's memoirs. Kersten took her at once to be a tourist. She was absorbed by what she read. When he glanced up he saw why. She had a tattoo on the inside of her forearm. The Nazis had given their concentration camp prisoners these very tattoos to identify them. Her number was 1033.

The stranger snapped the book shut and held it to her chest. She had decided to buy it. Kersten smiled ironically. *Oh, well. Good for her. She has suffered more than I can understand. Some of our best stories, our most comforting ones, are full of lies and must be. Besides, Bernadotte's day of reckoning shall come, as it does to every liar,* Kersten thought, as the woman turned and hit his shoulder. 'I'm so sorry,' she said lifting her dark eyes.

'Me too,' Kersten said. The woman stood staring at him. Her moist eyes sparkled and her jaw dropped. 'I feel like we've met somewhere before,' she said.

'In another life perhaps.' Kersten laughed good-naturedly.

'No, definitely in this one'.

The stranger raised her trembling hand. 'It was nice meeting you…'

'Felix Kersten.'

'No, I mustn't know you then…'

The lady smiled. She blushed and waved goodbye and went to the counter where she bought her book that the storekeeper gave to her in a bag. Kersten followed the strange woman with his eyes as she opened the door. 'Wait,' he said. 'You never told me your name.'

'Martine Belrose.'

Kersten tipped his hat and the woman left.

ABOUT THE AUTHOR

Jason Morgan is thirty eight years old and lives in Sydney, Australia. He is the author of two stories that appeared in Quadrant. His interest in literature began in his adolescence. Since then he has attended two universities, and he is presently enrolled in postgraduate studies. His interest in history and human nature inspired him to write about Felix Kersten who remains a largely obscure figure. Jason's other interests include music, cinema, and photography. He works as a librarian. This is his first novel.

www.ingramcontent.com/pod-product-compliance
Lightning Source LLC
Chambersburg PA
CBHW051826170626
46807CB00003B/1046